Penguin Fiction
The Affair

Hans Koning is now the pen name of Hans
Koningsberger, who was born in Amsterdam, Holland.
He studied at the University of Zurich, but he has been
writing in English ever since serving in the British Army
during the Second World War. Much of his life has
been spent in travel, but since 1951 he has made his
home in New York.

Four of his other novels, *An American Romance*,
A Walk With Love and Death, *The Revolutionary*, and
I Know What I'm Doing are also published in Penguins.
He has also written *Love and Hate in China*, *Along the
Roads of the New Russia*, *The Almost World* and the
Death of a Schoolboy. His play, *Hermione*, was shown
on the Continent in 1964, and he has written widely
for newspapers and magazines including the *New
Yorker*, the *New York Times*, the *Guardian* and *Punch*.
He has also helped write and produce films of some of
his books.

Hans Koning

The Affair

Penguin Books

Penguin Books Ltd, Harmondsworth,
Middlesex, England
Penguin Books Australia Ltd, Ringwood,
Victoria, Australia

First published in the U.S.A. by Alfred A. Knopf Inc. 1958
Published in Great Britain by Faber & Faber, 1959
Published in Penguin Books 1975

Made and printed in Great Britain by
C. Nicholls & Company Ltd
Set in Intertype Times

To Betita

He saw her for the first time on the late afternoon of the second of May. He was waiting at the exit of the Kursaal where a bazaar had been held. A friend of his had taken him there. She walked past him and waited also. She was alone and in a sudden impulse he asked her: 'Do you belong to somebody?'

She smiled and said that she didn't belong to anybody. A man walked up to them whose name was Jean-Pierre Day and whom they both knew. Her name was Catherine. It was in Zurich. More people came to stand and talk with them and they would all go and have dinner together somewhere in town.

He said that he might come later. He took the streetcar uphill with his friend, and they went home.

Later in the evening he came into their bar. They were still there, and he sat with them and drank Pernod too. She was wearing a bright yellow dress.

'Are you a student?' he asked her.

'I am a painter.' No, she couldn't say that she had a special style and she didn't believe in schools. She wanted to find her own form. She had not had an exhibition yet. She worked very hard.

'I am curious to see your work,' he said.

'We can do that sometime,' she answered.

'How did your face get that dark?' asked Day, 'do you take sunbaths?'

'I usually read on the roof at my place,' he murmured.

'Are you from Holland?' said a girl who had red hair and

wore a Lorraine cross on a chain round her neck. 'I thought that Dutchmen were blond.'

'Not all of them.'

As he walked home past the big extinguished windows of the shops and later past the still houses, he thought: Why do I never find anything to say? Why didn't I tell her how much I love painting, how much I think about it? I am not one of the lowly. Do you paint? What school if any? There is a stain on my tie. I am impossible. In his room he stared at the mirror and tried to see himself as she must have seen him. He went into the corridor to look up her name in the telephone directory.

He didn't know that she had hardly listened to him, that she had only once thought: He has nice hands. Ominous question: Do I belong to somebody? I guess I want to go home, I'd like to read in bed. Day is after all an irritating man.

*

The next morning he fell into a chair in Day's apartment and stared out of the window. Day shouted from the other room: 'Hello! I'll be with you. Isn't she charming? I have to go to the barber. Will you walk that far with me?'

'I have to work.'

He walked with him and he said to Day: 'She is very beautiful. She isn't in the telephone book.'

'What would you have wanted to tell her over the phone?'

'Nothing. I don't want anything.'

'Of course you do, Toni. Do you want to make love to her?'

'Don't be foolish,' Anthoni said, and smiled at him.

Day sat in the barber chair but he had not finished with the subject. He was French and looked it, with a rather large head and black gleaming hair, very regular features; he and Anthoni spoke English together. 'Ask her for dinner,' he told

Anthoni, who was leaning against a table and looking through the *Suisse illustrée*. 'The Schifflande, the second floor of course. Have good wine, not your Dôle, and buy her flowers. Build up a romantic scene, with style, my friend. Take her home, ask if you can come in, kiss her.'

'I am an especially poor student,' Anthoni said. 'Nor can I work such things, I wouldn't know what to talk about. I'd lie in bed afterwards and think of the things I should have said.'

'I assure you that every ...'

'And I don't believe in seductions with wine. You're dated.'

'She lives in an apartment house on Tal street, twenty I think.'

*

It was a day later when he telephoned her. He was sitting on the terrace of a café at the corner of the Limmat Quay, and at four o'clock he had decided to call her. At half past four he thought: It's a childish stupidity. She isn't waiting for me. I won't, I am going to a movie. There was a theatre on the other corner and its matinées started at three and five.

As soon as he had made that decision his peace of mind returned. At a quarter to five he suddenly got up from his table and went in to telephone.

I'll let it ring three times, he thought, then I'll hang up.

After the third ring a woman's voice answered and he asked for Miss Valois. A man came and stood in front of the booth, and he avoided his eyes.

'Catherine, it's me,' he said in a confused and hasty English, 'you said I could come and look at your paintings one day, could we make some sort of date?'

'Is it you? Thank you for your flowers.'

'Did you get them?'

'Why don't you pass by some evening after dinner? Not tonight, I won't be home.'

'May I come tomorrow night?'

'All right.'

He stepped out of the booth and looked back with a light

9

smile at everybody who looked at him as he pased through the
tables. He was happy that he had done it after all, that it had
worked, and really above all because nothing more had to be
done until tomorrow night. He had earned his movie now, he
had done his duty towards life, arranging an adventure of his
own and in reality. He bought a loaf of bread to eat out of the
wrapping-paper in the dark; he looked at the film love affair
and wondered as always where he would find the courage to
start a real one.

*

Zurich is two small rivers, and a lake, and a square and a circle
which are called Parade and Bellevue. On the fifth of May
1944, which was the year-to-be of the invasion of the German
continent, it was waiting, as were all towns and all cities of
Europe, and it was like a model town at a fair. It was white,
clean, small, and organized; it was a closely knit machine with
a little glass window through which to peek at a pre-war century. There was hunger in it but only the unpolitical and
national hunger of the very poor, and there was desolation but
it was the desolation of the fugitives. The quiet machine was
the Swiss town, and the international town was a second town.
There lived the fugitives – in the waiting void of the *visa for
the temporarily accepted* and the hours at the café Bali with
one coffee and ten magazines; the foreign students of the two
universities who were stranded, broke, and trying to be proud
of it; the spies, the consuls, the escaped Allied prisoners of
war, and the interned American pilots who had landed their
shot-up planes there; and the German Consul-General. The
international town was at war, many small wars, and it had
little communication with the Swiss town. The gasoline in
Switzerland was for the army, and both towns were without
automobiles. Riding across the Quay bridge on the streetcar,
one could hear the bells of the far church of the Fraumünster.

The sun was red through the gaps between the house roofs,
moving up along their row as the streetcar went around the
corner, and the lake shone greenly in the evening. In the quiet

10

light Anthoni walked to the door of the house in Tal street where he had never yet been, and he combed his hair in the glass before he pressed the bell.

*

It was a big house with wide silent corridors, and Catherine's apartment was on the third floor. There was a large room with two windows on the now darkened northern sky and her easel was standing near them. Catherine said that it was nice of him to have come; he said that it was nice of her to let him. His flowers were there, and she offered him a drink. There was a silence. He felt foolish; he had come to look at her pictures. How could he go on just sitting there, implying that she might now produce them for him? He was so much more aware of himself than of her; if he closed his eyes he would hardly know how she looked, but he was aware of his own clothes, of the frayed cuff on one leg of his trousers, and he had to resist the urge to comb his hair again. He waited, and he looked at her until they both smiled and she said: 'I am working on a sketch. Would you like to see it?'

It was a dark image, a court, a sort of patio, with light falling on a railing at the level of the second floor. There were two Spanish women dancing with closed eyes. 'They are dancing to the music which is coming from an inner room,' she said.

After that he looked at all the paintings that were standing in the room, facing the wall, and more which Catherine brought in from her bedroom. 'I have never sold anything ,' she said. 'I would like to, not for the money but to have them out of my rooms. They clutter my thoughts as long as they aren't gone.'

As they sat down Anthoni told her that he thought her work beautiful. He did, and saying it he suffered from the emptiness of those words. I'll say something clever about it, he thought, but I can't yet. I want to look more, I think that they are visions, which means to me: real paintings. I hate that school of art criticism which classifies everything in little jars.

He told her how he had been a student in Amsterdam and after the German invasion had tried to reach England through France and Spain. He had been arrested in France and just managed to escape to Switzerland; here he was living, like all the Dutch students in Zurich who were cut off from their families, on monthly loans granted by the consulate. But he did not want to stay in Switzerland; he wanted to get to England and join the British Army. He wanted that in a violent way. With the help of the Dutch Embassy it was possible to get through, but the embassy didn't do much and was, moreover, not too interested in his case since he had never had any military training. He had been told to continue his studies while waiting; but his time and thoughts were taken up by his efforts to get out, and his studies were by then not much more than an alibi for the Aliens' Police.

'Why are the police interested in you?' Catherine asked.

'Oh, this country is neutral, you know,' Anthoni answered. 'The Swiss don't want any allied activities going on here – you don't know what weird plans I've been working on, to contact French agents, get a false passport out of some South American consul, things like that . . .' I mustn't pursue this, Anthoni thought, I'd talk about my heroic deeds for an hour and make a fool of myself, she can't be interested in all this; but he tried to put something in his voice when he spoke about waiting for England, something of the nostalgia for that country where he had never been. England seemed a land of light to him, and when he saw an English newsreel or a month-old *Tatler* flown in from Sweden that emotion overwhelmed him and he would stare endlessly at the photograph of a Spitfire, at the faces of soldiers.

'I was in school in England for two years,' Catherine said. 'I wonder whether I'd like to be there now . . . yes, I guess I would if I were a man. Everything is so inane here, this city does not do anything for you, it doesn't add to your mood.'

"Aren't you going to stay here after the war?'

'Oh, never. As soon as this is over I'm going to live and work in Paris.'

'As soon as this is over' annoyed Anthoni and he fell silent and looked at her. Catherine had dark hair, falling in waves, tied at the back with a ribbon, her wide eyes seemed grey in the light. Here I am, he thought, this is me, me sitting on a couch in Zurich next to a very beautiful woman. I don't think I have ever been in quite this situation; translated into words it sounds so very exciting. Why do I need the words? I do want an adventure, I ache for one; I should kiss her, but I do not dare to. When his vague thoughts had reached that point, Catherine put out her hand and let it glide gently over his hair 'You have nice hair,' she said. What do I do now, what do I do now, Anthoni thought, but his thoughts were passed by his movements and he leaned over to her and kissed her. Her mouth was large and soft, and when he touched her he closed his lips tightly and sucked in his breath so that his kiss would be dry. That's all he was thinking as he kissed Catherine Valois. She kissed him back and she did not look at him and stood up and walked to the window.

*

There was the sensation which Anthoni called for himself the 'dropping in time and in space' and into which he let himself glide when he was lying in bed and waiting to fall asleep. He thought of far time and of far place, and it was the doubleness of the void between these and himself which made him reel. He thought of the caravan halting at nightfall three thousand years ago by the wall of Samarkand, and of the Hindu king who made his villagers build the Burubudur temple in what was for Europe the ninth century; and getting lost in the immense spaciousness exhilarated him. Then too there was the imagining of himself fleeing, running for life in a city, with nothing but the clothes he had on, how he would escape by hiding first in a movie theatre, then under a bridge, how he would live in the woods, escape to Africa, to Asia. He conjured up the actuality of the Swiss police knocking at this, his bedroom door, and how he would manage to climb into the gutter, down to the ground, how he would then make for the funicular railway and hide in the bushes, glide down along its rails through the grass, and run to the Schifflande bar where he would ask the girl Thea, who would still be there, alone, counting the receipts, to hide him.

So he dreamed all the way and all the details from the gutter of his rooming-house in Culmann street across the border of Switzerland, and then to a Spanish freighter and the African continent, possessing nothing, hunted but free, with the whole earth to go. And he let himself fall down in time and he was a Spanish adventurer, a disinherited student, landing in the Americas; and he wandered among the Indians, and raped a wild nude girl. He dreamed of women, imaginary women, and he saw himself in harems and in medieval courts, and then he looked at himself walking along the streets on a summer night and thinking: I am desiring so much, and somewhere there must be a woman desiring like me, without fulfilment; and if we could only find each other, if we could only be drawn together, if you could put a message in the paper, a notice in which you said that you were available to fulfil somebody's desire and thus fulfil your own.

And he thought of a girl who had let him make love to her. She had been the first, she had seduced him more than he her, and the dark dream he had of in-ness was from a different world than that in which he had her. Lying in bed waiting for her, he would feel an unbearable passion, and when she was there he would become aware all of a sudden of other feelings, pains, urges; he would feel uncomfortable, afraid, and glad when it was over, hoping that she, though discontented, would yet let him alone.

*

Anthoni got up and went slowly to the window, not looking out, and stood next to Catherine and kissed her in her hair. She turned her head under and away from him and kissed him on his mouth and touched his teeth with her tongue.

He was now dominated by that strange idea that it was his, male, duty to go on, to be ahead always of what she implied she wanted, a chivalry of wanting, stronger and less inhibited

14

than that of the other, the woman. She had closed her eyes, and he lifted her, took a step with her in his arms, and then said in a difficult, soft voice: 'Left or right?' Left was back to the couch where they had been and right was to her bedroom.

'Right,' she answered, later to tell him that she had meant not the bedroom, but that is was all right as it had been.

She had left the door open after bringing in her paintings, and he entered that room and carried her to the bed and sat on the edge stroking her hair away from her face. This is silly and like a film, he had thought as he carried her, but it had really been a natural movement, and without effort. But now, bending over her, he felt self-conscious and alarmed for his body seemed dull and passionless. This was a dreamed and desired situation but he would like to escape and the sentence leaped through his head: I wish that the phone would ring, or somebody come and knock. He closed his eyes and slowly felt for a button of her blouse.

Catherine said: 'You must wait. I must tell you something, and I want to lie still for a few minutes before I do. Do you mind?'

He kissed her without saying anything. He walked out of the room and across the corridor to where he had seen the bathroom, and then came back and locked the apartment door behind him, put out the light and dropped his jacket and his tie on a chair and left his shoes on his way through the dimly lit room, and lay down very gently beside her.

She said: 'Do you know what plastic surgery is? I had an operation on my breasts when I was eighteen. They were too big, and it was something like plastic surgery. It left a scar under them, and I wanted to tell you before you see it, and I want to know if you mind.'

He took off her blouse and kissed her breasts and said: 'They are so beautiful, how could you think such a thing?' He looked at her body, which was supple and lovely, he came to her, and she didn't say anything but: oh, and then it was over for him, very quickly.

Beside her he murmured: 'Please forgive me. It will be

better, it's because it is the first time.' She smiled at him and said: 'Yes, I know. Your body looks just as I thought it would. I want to paint you one day. Please close your eyes.'

She got up and washed, put on a gown and went out, came in again and sat on the bed. 'I have a friend,' she said, 'and you know, I could never start a thing like this. You are a very sweet man, but it was for this once only.'

*

Woods surrounding Switzerland were inhabited by men, men living on the stone-cold slopes of the Italian Alps and in the copse which covers the arid hills of French Provence and is called *maquis*. The Maquis who took their name from the undergrowth out of which they went to forage at night, stealing from lonely farmlands and pens, out at night to destroy the trains and the works of the Germans, and climbing back before dawn to sleep, or suffer from wounds during the day when the heat of the sun penetrated the thick and damping shrub. A ghostly ring of men who were covered in the rear by a land of vacuous neutrality, with messengers to form the unbelievable link between their woods and the lit streets, theatregoers, so very few miles from each other.

A messenger took the streetcar to Eaux-Vives on a rainy Geneva evening and stood on the front platform to the end of the line. The lights of the shops were reflected in the empty streets where a few people hurried home. He walked with his hands pushed through his pockets, holding the parcels inside his raincoat, past yards where coal was stacked, a guardhouse, a shuttered café on a corner; and then the houses receded and he walked through fields, stopping to fasten his collar more tightly against the rain, the city lights in the sky at his back, treading along the street of Eaux Vives, a last street light swaying over the road from a crosswire, and then a path only, a left turn before a powerhouse. He walked in the dark over the dirt path, then over the grass and stones, going slower and slower through the hours, with his mud-filled shoes, and in an endless weariness. He was carrying French money bought that morning at the marble window of the Caisse Genevoise, twelve Swiss army pistols, a paper bag with Cibazol for wounds and vitamins and chocolate, a bottle of rum for himself, and a novel. Thus was the link, and thus he went on until he came to the barbed wire between Switzerland and German France, where he listened for steps and for dogs, then crept under it and past it and walked to be shot or to reach the bush before dawn ended the night of rain.

*

This morning was blue with sunlight over the Zurich lake, falling over the lawn shore and through the white pillars of Bellevue Palace, around which the streetcars circle before they climb up the hill-streets or cross the river, a white circle where people wait and sit and buy their papers, a circle to stand on and look over the water, look into the sun and be happy with the newness of the day and of your life. It was now five days ago that he had met Catherine Valois, and the day before yesterday that he had seen her and made love to her; yesterday a day of thinking of her body, her eyes, of a desire which he felt then, not when he was lying next to her; he told himself that he had fallen in love with her, and already while thinking that, he knew how it was not so, how he just, just wanted an adventure, an honour done him, a dropping into a new society; and then wondered whether 'falling in love' was always that, whether it was only an emotion learned from books.

He was to see her again now, and it was his vanity, his *amour-propre*, which made his throat dry, which made him look in the glass next to the newspaper stand to scrutinize himself, avoiding the eyes of the salesman who leaned over the counter. He saw her coming across the glittering street, in a coat of vivid green, and she looked so beautiful, there was such precision in her beauty, that he felt a wonder in her directing herself towards him, and her once having accepted him seemed unthinkable, more unthinkable still his having taken her, having shown her his body.

*

Just before she reached him this sensation was so over-whelming that his vision was almost blacked out – a grey veil drew over the outside world and his whole being seemed to push towards that goal of assertion which was: to remain, to keep this place in her life which an ephemeral caprice had given him two days ago.

'Hello, how are you,' he said. 'It was very sweet of you to let me come with you to the exhibition.'

And he walked at her side along the lake shore to an art-dealer's place where a painter named Linsenmayer had an-nounced an exhibition of his work.

There were gigantic butterflies, caterpillars, and spiders, and in the too clear visibility of each detail of their bodies, hairs, joints, spots was the nightmare of your eyes popping out, of seeing too much, the old frightful dream of the corpse visible through the trunk in which it was hidden.

'He terrifies me,' Anthoni said. 'His name is wonderfully appropriate.'

That was because Linsenmayer was a German name and Linsen means lenses, and yet that heavy remark seemed sharp, his sombre voice showed that he had not intended it to be funny; and this lenses boy seemed a ghostly pseudonym for someone who saw too much and did not keep his terrible secrets.

Why is this so frightening? Anthoni thought, and he contin-ued: 'I guess we can live in this world in sanity only because we do not look too closely at the details.'

'You have good judgement for painting,' she said.

'I meant to say that we have dusted out the corners,' Anthoni hastened on, 'and that there are lights now behind the curtains and under the bed. Oh the heavens are so dark that we certainly need a well-lit earth. We're sort of living in a screened house. Real reality is intolerable. Even a little piece like Linsenmayer.'

Catherine smiled faintly, she seemed to wait for him to say more.

'I don't care,' Anthoni said, and he thought of the sunlight over the streets and the wideness of that day and of the world. What did it all matter to him? 'Not on a day like this. But it's true. I'll tell you, I saw a film once, Bob Hope in Africa, he gets into a cave full of skeletons, or something like that, his fright is a joke. People want such a thing, they need it now. You can't have people dying any more, not in a world of faster cars and bigger sales. I must sound confused, do you understand what I mean? The terror of death must be taken away, there is too much to live for. The Germans do it the other way around. They can't stand too good a life.'

'I think you're right about your Bob Hope,' Catherine said gravely. 'But not about insanity when you put out the light. These spiders are not the real reality. That's what you science people think. They are not my reality. Death is a shadow, and a vital one. It is the shadow which puts life into relief. How could you paint without it?'

'I think people would be quite willing to give up painting,' Anthoni replied.

'I'd rather do without your physics,' Catherine said, frowning.

*

'Don't be too obscure my friend,' Day said. 'You did make love to her then. It is something to be happier about, she is a very special woman.'

'Yes, once,' Anthoni murmured. 'And she told me it could never happen again. But it did, yesterday.'

He was almost inaudible as he spoke, as if he were trying not quite to talk about it. A thing he never had done, never would do, yet he could not resist it. There was an elation in the understatement of his murmured sentences, and in the giving of reality, anew, to Catherine who again had grown so vague. Yesterday afternoon he had left her house, thirty-six hours ago, gone along the street in the bright straight light and felt a chosen man, walking among the people who were thinking of business, shopping, he coming from Catherine's bed. He had gone to his room and tried vainly to read, left again and was on the street, feeling happy in his unseenness by her, nothing to keep up, no effort of being or seeming; his haggardness now of no concern, nobody else to win, a slumming in one's self. Then the light began to withdraw from the town, he was walking on Bahnhof street, groups of passers-by brushing him, and he stopped to look in the gleaming shop-windows, rows of books, flowers, the sky paling when he looked straight upwards along the fronts of the houses. He wanted to speak to her, telephone her, say a few words, but then he did not, wishing to keep this thing, this feeling, whole, unexposed, in himself, nursing the thought without touching it.

He had awakened late the following morning and putting something on, gone into the corridor, closing the door to his landlady's living-room, and called her up. He had not thought of it beforehand, knowing that thinking would stop him. Miss Valois wasn't in, the girl answered.

He had left his number but then he had dressed hurriedly in an urge to get out of the house, putting a roll in his pocket, some books under his arm, hastily closing the door behind him, and down the stairs, consciously not listening to the telephone which might ring just then. At four he had called his house. There had been no messages for him.

'Two more beers, Miss,' Day said. 'I guess I envy you, Toni. When I'm honest I must confess to some sort of regret. I wish I had tried. But I don't think I'm her type. You surprise me pleasantly.' And he looked at Anthoni, scrutinizing his face, his hands, with a sober and calculating expression in his eyes.

'Why don't you take the other room in my apartment, Toni?' Day continued. 'Don't you think its a nice place? We can split the rent.'

Anthoni said, smiling: 'I think you'll never believe that there really are people who live on two hundred and twenty francs a month. That's what I do. Ask the consul. I can't split any rents, Jean-Pierre.'

'Well, stay with me tonight anyway, if you feel like it. I

don't think you'd still find a tram. Do you approve of the waitress? I want to ask her something.'

It was past midnight in the Corso, a big place one block from the lake, in the heart of the small centre which was night-time Zurich. They weren't sitting in the main hall where there had been dancing earlier in the evening and which was closed now, but in a side restaurant, glaring light, a few people, late-returning salesmen eating bread with sausage, wooden tables with beer felts.

The waitress came over and Jean-Pierre Day spoke to her softly. She shook her head and walked a few steps away

'I asked her whether she wears a brassière," Day said. 'She said no.'

At the far end of the restaurant the lights went out and chairs were being put on the tables.

'My friend and I and some other people are going to have a small party in my apartment,' Day suddenly almost shouted in his brightly unorthodox German. 'Won't you join us?'

'Oh, you know, I'm very tired,' the waitress said.

'It's right around the corner, Seefeld street, it's really going to be very nice and quiet, and we won't make it too late. And this charming man here will come too. Tell her to come, Toni.'

Anthoni reacted only with a slight smile at the waitress in which was something of the amused superiority he felt at that moment over Jean-Pierre. The thought that he would become an accomplice in this, one of Day's wild stories, did not please him.

The waitress did not smile back at him and she said to Day: 'All right, I'm coming. You have to wait ten minutes.'

They walked to Day's apartment along the dim and empty Seefeld street, Day now calling the waitress *mon petit chou* without any reaction from her; Anthoni walking a step behind, looking at her ankles which buckled a little over her grey shoes, slightly worn heels, and then breathing deeply in a sudden mist of heavy-heartedness.

The waitress did look surprised when Jean-Pierre's apartment turned out to be devoid of any party crowd, but she did not seem unduly alarmed and took no notice of Anthoni's faint apology when he left the room.

He undressed in the big cold room which Day left unused, put his clothes on a chair at the window and fell into bed, rolling himself as well as possible in the blankets which were too small to reach all the sides.

Soon afterwards he heard Day say to her in the corridor: 'Won't you go and say good night to my friend too?'

Anthoni muttered a protest to himself, he would never want, never dare to do that, but his mouth became dry and his heart beat in his throat. Then he heard the front door slam, and Day came into his room.

'Easy come, easy go,' he said in a jaunty voice. 'I gave her twenty francs and she seemed pleased.'

'What did she say when you asked her to have that look at me too?'

'She only shook her head.'

'It was a short party all right. Is she beautiful? Aren't you afraid to get a dose from those things?'

'A dose?' Day said with the slightly amazed smile he often had for Anthoni.

'I thought you had been a lieutenant.'

'French officers speak slightly differently from British sergeants, my friend.'

'I wish I were one all the same.'

'She had nice hard breasts, she really doesn't need a bra. I knew, I looked when I asked her. It's a vital point. Are you sure you don't want to take this room? You can pay me in pounds or something.'

'It's bloody cold here,' Anthoni said. 'I have no pounds either. Good night. When will you get me out of here, Jean-Pierre, to England, to your Maquis?'

'I might want to go myself. I'm trying for you.'

Anthoni felt relieved because there had been no temptation for him, but this thought was divided. Why hadn't she come in; when you went for parties of that kind you might as well take forty francs home instead of twenty. Not that he would have had twenty francs for her.

Jean-Pierre must have known that, he had obviously intended to treat him. One round on the house. Day hadn't looked happy at all with his adventure A rather sad and lonely thing for a man who wanted to be about-town. More for the benefit of the gallery? A good thing that he couldn't afford this room. There was possibly more freedom with a Culmann-street landlady than as Day's private gallery.

*

Late Sunday afternoon, five o'clock, darkness falling outside, no lamps lit yet in the room, was a dream which lived in Anthoni, a childhood image which was a translation of all fears and melancholy. He did not know whether that afternoon, his symbol of sadness – the fathomlessness of the world, the fear of living in an old and empty house on a vast moor – had really happened or was a diffused picture built by himself. Five o'clock on a Sunday afternoon, he was sitting on a chair, far from the window, he was a child and he was staring at a schoolbook, the lesson for tomorrow. There was an old-fashioned drawing of a fox over the text and the lesson was titled *Le Renard*. It was silent, his brother was at the table, his mother was reading, they had been for a walk, the silence and the isolation of Amsterdam on a November Sunday. He had avoided looking when they passed the medical-instrument shop on the Rokin which had a skull in the window, and he had felt sick.

The French book, the medical shop, and there was a visit too, that day?, to the Safety Museum where there were pictures of mutilated workmen and how to prevent such things and of the liver of an alcoholic and how much milk a bottle of gin would buy, a horror which was almost dreary, like the murals of square-faced men and women who held hammers and bushels of wheat on the walls of the municipal clinic – all that an image against the windows of that room and the fading light in the street outside.

23

And then the dream of the sea, the ocean, the green mass of water, so high, so high, and ships descending through it, bodies of the sailors who had drowned from their torpedoed ships, who floated in midwater, thousands of feet of water over them and under them, enveloped in an endless ocean, the darkness of the undermost layers, silent monster fish, bones of the men who had drowned so long ago, knights in armour. The fear and yet the abandonment of drowning, submerging in one element.

*

Robert Ellis was the first American Anthoni had ever known. He was in his forties but seemed younger, and with his tanned face and dark hair and moustache he had the appearance of an Italian nobleman. He had indeed spent most of his life in Italy, and as an American he was so little of a specimen that in their debates on Americanism Anthoni found himself in the role of defender of the faith. A faith he had from his books, from a university course on United States history, a faith which had to be, because it was in harmony with what then seemed to him to be the essence of the just war, as he had named it for himself.

There was so much death that scepticism was no longer sophisticated; there were wild feelings in him about the men drafted from all countries to liberate Europe; and when Ellis spoke of New York which was too crowded, too high-strung and too dirty to live in, Anthoni laughed superiorly. How did he know, Ellis asked; but Anthoni's thoughts were of a non-existent land of Penn and De Tocqueville.

It was an unequal debate, for Ellis was not one of those who have gone to Europe in frustration; he was member of a vanishing group of a vanishing age, living in a class and not in a country. And yet Anthoni felt himself considered by Ellis the better man, because he believed and had given himself the right to believe by his own life, his escape from Holland, his future enlistment in the British army: the unanswerable, ennobling argument.

'We haven't seen you in a long time,' Ellis said. 'What have you been doing with yourself?'

'Working, wandering,' Anthoni answered in a vague voice. 'You must forgive me for butting in on your brunch, if such forgiveness is possible.'

Ingeborg said: 'Only for you, Toni, but not even for you if you don't sit down here immediately. You are making me nervous, and you are too tall. I can't eat in your shadow.'

'I'm sitting,' Anthoni murmured, and he continued: 'It's the tenth of May. Holland has been at war for four years today. 10 May 1940, I've never gotten up so early as that day, Inge.'

'Please don't call me Inge,' Ingeborg said. 'If you want to have brunch, you must have it on our terms, which means: silently. And have an egg unless you want to imply that the situation is too grim for such things.'

'I can eat an egg without giving it a thought,' Anthoni answered. 'I'm still. I'll read your movie magazines.'

'Germany is just as much an occupied country as Holland,' Ingeborg said.

'It's not, because the Germans are happy about it all.'

'I'm not happy about it.'

'But that's why they took your passport away'

Ingeborg had come from Germany to Switzerland two years earlier because of tuberculosis and had lost her nationality when she refused to go back after the treatment. Just before the war, as a girl, she had begun to play in German films. She and Ellis had a furnished apartment in Flora street, near the lake.

'Don't look so angrily at me,' Anthoni went on, 'please don't think I do not know how hard it is to be stuck here without nationality and without their bloody permits A, B, and C ... I know, but admit you're an exception. I don't believe Hitler is moving history. He is riding a wave. He is a child of Nietzsche.'

That made Ingeborg furious. 'There is nothing more exasperating than people talking about things they don't know anything about,' she cried. 'Have you ever read one line of his? Don't talk like a refugee professor in a B-movie, I beg you.'

'But I did read him, you know,' Anthoni said. 'As much as I could stand of it. I believe that there is something in his mentality, and in the average German mentality, that is wrong – wrong because it doesn't fit in the modern world. *L'esprit boche*, a violence, a primitive sentiment that force is more glamorous than ideas.'

'I don't believe there is such a thing as the average man in any country,' Robert Ellis answered him. 'I have seldom met a German I liked, but I do think you oversimplify things, Toni. Don't your people use violence in your colonies? And the English? Not that we are any better. What's the difference between killing Jews and killing Red Indians?'

'Don't be so objective,' Anthoni said. 'You're right, you're right, but you are so very wrong to be objective in May 1944. Do you know how many casualties England already has? Do you know that twenty thousand English sailors have drowned up till now? Hasn't that washed away the past? Those men didn't want anything but to be left in peace. We can't sit here after our lunch and come up with colonies and Indians. You don't mean to say that you're in doubt as to who started it this time? I really have no illusions about any big power, but there are differences. Do you know that some German in Poland said: "For the first time in history we are going to make absolute use of a military victory, and Poland will vanish from the earth"? Oh come on now, you . . .'

Anthoni stopped himself. Ellis had lived in Italy ever since he went to Milan as a young man to study engineering. In 1941 he had been interned when the United States entered the war, and a year later he had been allowed to go to Switzerland. Anthoni could not forgive him all those years he had obviously lived so at ease under Mussolini. Ellis was completely invulnerable on the subject. He said that he certainly hadn't approved, but that those things looked different in Italy from the way they did to outsiders. On such occasions his smile implied that Anthoni would learn later that one country wasn't any better than another, and there seemed almost a nostalgia in his expression for Anthoni's age when the world was divided into black and white.

'You know what, Toni,' Ingeborg said suddenly, and she got up from the couch on which she used to sit propped up with pillows while eating, 'let's go to *King's Row* at three. Robbie doesn't want to see it. It's in Selnau, I don't want to go alone.'

'Oh, I'm so sorry,' Anthoni answered in a hesitating voice. 'I'd like to see that with you. But I have to be somewhere at five and I couldn't make it.'

'Can't you phone and make that six?'

'I'd really like to, but it is impossible.' Anthoni reddened slightly, and they both looked at him half smiling.

'Please let me take you there, though,' he continued.

Ingeborg frowned.

*

The dark water of the Sihl hurried over the stone dam in the river, reflecting the big clouds which filled up the afternoon sky, vanishing rapidly under the bridge; there was a side path which followed the stream from the stone balustrade of the bridge to where it ended against a wall, and there was a cast-iron bench by it. A newspaper was lying on the ground and Anthoni held it with his feet, bending over to look at the page, and started reading a column on a municipal building-project, stopped and looked at the people, streetcars, crossing the bridge. Selnau, I will never live in streets like these, he thought. I am poor enough, I can be poorer for sure, but never this. Nobody has to, I believe, it makes you feel grey, dirty – yet to wander around unshaven, in old clothes, not seen by anyone who knows you, there is a warmth in that, the warmth of belonging. If you are poor you always belong. A big indoor swimming-pool, 'today for men' it said on a prim Swiss sign, a cafeteria, a greyness as in *Metropolis*, Ingeborg would have to take the streetcar home alone. He would have liked to see the film now.

The feeling of uneasiness which he had suppressed in his

vague stream of thoughts, yet knowing it was there, now came to the surface. At five o'clock he was going to Catherine's house to take her out for a drink. It was his idea, she had seemed to hesitate when he called; he felt clumsy and excited and tired. The wretched hope that something big would happen, something terrible, to give him a frame—Switzerland at war, he would run to her house, feel strong, needed. A poor wish.

He went into the cafeteria, down the steps to the men's room, looked at himself and feared his lack of wanting. He straightened his shirt, his tie, combed his hair, made it stick to the back of his head with water, washed his hands and left the tap running, and went back up, past the tables, out. It was only four o'clock.

*

He just touched her hand as a greeting. She was painting, in a grey linen smock buttoned at the back, her hair up, frowning, surprised that it was five. She looked out of her window over the back gardens and at the dark light in the sky

'I'm sorry I am not dressed,' she said. 'I hope you don't mind waiting.'

'Of course not,' Anthoni murmured with a smile, looking at her and at her painting, which was of herself sitting upright in a red velvet chair. 'I have interrupted you.'

'No, I have to stop,' Catherine answered. 'I am glad you came, I want to get out of here Play some music if you want to. The phonograph isn't very good. I have to go and buy a new one. Perhaps you can come with me some day.'

They walked rather silently along Tal street with its solid houses, crossed the heavier traffic and were caught in some filtered sunlight when they went across the bridge over the Limmat. Anthoni felt a weight on his mind, his thoughts and his words seemed so ponderous, unwieldy, and the little city under the sky of clouds seemed a silence, a massive surrounding. He thought again of that sterile, outrageous wish for a frame created by the excitement of brutal outward happenings.

28

As a schoolboy once at a party, sitting with a girl, he had felt so dumbstruck that he had had that hope, thinking, oh I wish there would be a fire, a fight.

So often had he felt himself to have a great mind that a vexation sometimes seized him when he read a critic's praise of someone; realizing the petty reaction, yet musing: if they only knew, if they only knew all the things which stir in me, which wait to be communicated. He seemed to have no time then to start on that slow communication; it seemed intolerable that one more day should pass without the world knowing that he was not just another one of the public, of the waiting-to-be told. Somewhere related to this had been the necessity of choosing for his field what had seemed the most difficult and boring but the most final science, physics. Here he walked over the flat stones of the embankment and thought: I wish a friend would pass and greet me, a drunk accost us.

He said: 'I wish we were in Paris.' Yes, perhaps he was going to live there later, he answered her, and said to himself: How? I have to finish my physics, God, three more years as a student, where? In Zurich or in Holland, how else could I manage? Commute to Paris from the university here. But then, first there is the war, I'll get to be an officer, things will be easy afterwards, money has lost its absoluteness, I can only hope to be alive when it is all over. And he experienced a strange joy about the wild tumult in the world around them, which stopped only at the borders of Switzerland and he looked at Catherine and said: 'Where else? It's the heart of the world.'

*

It was because his father had a grain-importing business in Lausanne that Day, a reserve lieutenant in the French army, had been able to go to Switzerland after the debacle of France. Living now in Zurich, he only occasionally showed up in the Lausanne office where there was hardly anything going on anyway; he was no man of business, he always said. There were few Frenchmen of his circle in Switzerland then: some of the very wealthy who had managed the funds and the papers to escape from the ever more meagre French suppers to the basic solidity of Switzerland; a few who continued the war they had lost earlier and had chosen that country for their headquarters. These last were Day's people, for he was on their side. There was too much civilization in Day for him to be attracted by the derailed rich and the frustrated young men who formed French collaborationism. It was no sophistry which had made him stop short of actually joining the Maquis. There were many humps in his being he could not lift himself over, and he was seldom bothered by that. Easy come, easy go was usually enough for him as a battle cry. Yet there was a simpleness in this which made him acceptable.

When he heard from his father that Lennard, an old friend of his, had come to Geneva from France, he took a late morning train and went to talk to him.

It was a big house in Danton street which is one of the still and wide, tree-bordered streets in the southern section of Geneva. A staircase with an old but thick carpet; Lennard's room was on the second floor, its windows looking out on the foliage of a tree. The early summer air carried vague sounds.

'They say that this is a French city,' Pierre Lennard said. 'And they are terribly wrong. I am always surprised when the shopgirls and the waiters understand me. Geneva has a Swiss culture, and the Swiss culture is basically German. It is very close to your Zurich, and it is very far from Paris.'

'It must have been more French once,' Day supposed, 'when borders didn't matter so much yet. And before this war. The Swiss struck France from their record, my friend, in 1940. As if she had been a questionable hotel guest. The room clerk gets orders to ignore her or tell her the hotel is all filled up.'

'I guess by now they are beginning to realize that they may have been too quick. France will be liberated this year. A lot of the liberating is going on right now, by ourselves.'

Day said: 'Do you have anything to drink in the house? I don't want to go out yet, do you? I wonder what you think of me, you sitting here after a stretch in the woods, and talking to me who in that time was shaved every morning by the same barber in the Seefeld *strasse*.'

'As a matter of fact, I don't know why I am not more disgusted with you,' Pierre said and smiled at Day. 'Soldiers are supposed to hate civilians, and I have certainly done my share of soldiering, and a bit too much.'

'I wonder whether I should go with you next time,' Day said.

'It might be an idea. But don't do it because you think you have to. I won't be less happy to have a drink with you afterwards. I am sure you are an impressive client in your barber-shop. You are, after all, part of the civilization we are defending.'

Day smiled sourly.

'Well, and damn it all, that isn't so silly,' Pierre cried. 'I'm sure that when you order a special massage à la this or that, you do more to restore your barber's faith in the future of France than all the speeches of De Gaulle, if he would listen to them.'

Day felt his head as if to ascertain whether he was in need of any massaging. 'I guess I'm getting old,' he murmured. 'A friend of mine, a nice chap, would give his soul to get to England and be a soldier.'

'How old is he?' Pierre asked.

'Twenty-one, I think. No military experience.'

'Not French?'

'No.'

'It's an enormous risk we take every time we guide somebody through France,' Pierre said, 'even if he is completely trustworthy. If he's caught the Germans roll up a whole line through him. It must be very important to get a man to England, important for our war, before we'd consider it.'

'I know.'

'Where is he from actually?'

'Holland. When the Germans invaded he managed to get himself on a line through France but he ran into trouble and ended up in Switzerland. He really wants to get into that army, he's been driving the entire diplomatic corps crazy, and me too,' Jean-Pierre said in an amused voice.

'Well, you can always let him write me through you, don't you think? A letter about his ideas?'

*

After their drink Anthoni had taken Catherine to the house where she was to attend a dinner party, a sort of family affair she said, and she had answered a hesitation in him when he wished her good night by asking him to have lunch with her. 'If you come to my place tomorrow, we can eat in my room,' she said. 'They serve meals, rather good.'

In the morning he went to the university at nine and left at ten to go back to his room. He could not go straight to Catherine from somewhere else, she could not be a second station on the road, he had to go back to his base first, think, wash, clean his shoes, a refuelling of vanity. It was not precisely that, it was an urge in him not to be anything less with her than the utmost possible – an acute awareness of himself, of how he looked, spoke; and he went to her after endless preparation. He did not consider his motives, he just did not bother to do that. He knew that there was no love in him, but the idea that she might return to those original words, never again, was shattering.

When he came into her room, Catherine was playing a record. She had been working on her self-portrait, but now it stood on the easel with its back turned; she wore her grey coat and a ribbon in her hair.

'Hello,' he said, 'how lovely you look this morning.' Catherine smiled at him with a radiance he had not seen on her face before. 'Thank you,' she answered. 'Come sit on the couch with me and I'll ring for the maid.'

The girl came and served them, and they ate from big, white china plates.

'The dinner party was dreadful,' Catherine said afterward. 'I have never felt so restless. I was home at eleven. I almost phoned you to come over.' 'I am so sorry you didn't,' Anthoni answered her, 'I was thinking of you.' Catherine moved until she was sitting close to him, against him. She put her left arm around his neck and pulled his head towards her and kissed him, and then let herself glide backward until her head rested on the arm of the couch, away from him. He caressed her, first through the smock, then under it, and she sighed, moving her body with his hands.

Then she groaned almost inaudibly and pressed his hands with hers. She lay quite still, and opened her eyes wide, smiled at him, and said in a sunny voice: 'Oh, how lovely. Thank you.' Anthoni did not answer, but leaned his head back and closed his eyes. He was very excited and he hoped that she would notice, but she jumped up, looked out of the window, turned her painting around and said, as if to herself: 'I feel so clear now, I want to work like a madwoman.' Anthoni sat quite still, and his excitement subsided to leave him with a terrible feeling of emptiness and being spent He looked at her with a wry face and murmured something in annoyance. Catherine came over to him and touched his hair. 'You can come tonight if you wish,' she said softly.

She had a wide bed which smelled of her perfume, and he looked at her hair and face in the pillow. He had come to her feeling fearful and empty after an afternoon in which he had kept telling himself that he had to shake out his self-doubts and come back to her with less intentness; he had had it very quickly and had said: 'Please wait,' and she was now lying with her head on his arm. 'Tell me about yourself,' he asked.

'What do you want to know?'

'Everything you know yourself. Tell me about the first time you made love. How old were you then?'

'I was eighteen,' Catherine said with a laugh in her voice. 'I was rather ugly, I think. It was in a hotel in Gstaad.'

'What happened?' Anthoni asked, and his heart beat faster, and there was an old sickening sensation in him.

'Oh, I stayed there with my sister. There was a Frenchman and I had a drink with him and we danced, and in the middle of the night he knocked on my door.'

'Did you let him in?'

'Yes, don't sound so amazed. I was curious. I told him I was a virgin. I didn't want him, not in me. So we just lay there and stroked each other, and then I kissed him here.' And she touched Anthoni.

'Catherine, not really?' Anthoni asked her, 'the first time you saw a man? Weren't you frightened?'

Catherine smiled at him. 'No, Toni. It excited me as much as it did him.'

'Catherine, you are the most amazing woman I have ever heard of.' Anthoni felt shocked, breathless, a painful jealousy of that man. What was wrong in him that it seemed more desirable to be taken by Catherine than to take her? He looked at her, he moved his hands over her body and went to kiss her. She was quicker than he this time.

He woke up because the light was on. Catherine said: 'I am so sorry, dear, but you have to go home.'

'Oh, Cath,' Anthoni said, 'can't I stay the whole night with you?'

'It's really impossible, Toni. They would see you go out. The maid comes in to fix the room.'

'Couldn't I wait until it is light?'

'Oh yes. It's half past three now.'

'Lord,' Anthoni murmured, 'I might as well go home now.' He felt exhausted, he dressed with closed eyes and then sat down on the floor next to her bed. 'I'm so sleepy,' he said and let his head rest against the sheet. After a few minutes he opened his eyes again and looked at her. 'Good night, dear girl,' he said and moved his hand over her hair. She looked very simple and young, her head, her round shoulders in a nightgown with lace edges; and he had slept next to her. He

felt a disproportionate sadness in going away and thought:
how lovely to share your nights with a woman. He said:
'Catherine I love you.' She brought out her hand from under
the covers and offered it to him to be kissed. He left, opened
the door to look out at the empty corridor, went very quietly
down the stairs and then closed the front door behind him. As
soon as it was closed he stepped out hard in the night, and
started what was almost a march, putting his feet down with a
thud on the sidewalk. It was a long way up to his Culmann-
street bed. He felt jubilant.

*

The two-sided echo of your steps in an empty street, from
corner to corner. The streets are cool under a pale sky, as if
waiting for the morning, the walls are warm and cover the
shuttered sleeping rooms. The knowledge of yourself, the rare
emotion of I am I.

The feeling, too, of a belonging, unexplainable in this city
because the real inhabitants of Zurich he did not know nor
wish to know; that feeling he had christened: traffic-light feeling, because there was an image in him of himself as a boy,
waiting on his bicycle for a traffic light on an Amsterdam
square, the mass of people all around him, nobody he knew,
nobody who knew him, but a warmth surging through him
suddenly, which was a loving of everybody. The naturalness of
sitting there on his bicycle with his foot on the ground, like all
the others, everyone understanding and recognizing that
moment, everyone waiting for the light to change to go home.

And that other feeling, of your self, which was more than
this traffic-light belonging. More, or the opposite? Coming out
of school on a winter night, under the street lights, suddenly
sinking and feeling: I am I, see yourself go, feel as if you were
a little man in your own head, looking out through your eyes,
an intense emotion of aloneness in the endless world, awaiting
death; then it was over again and only remembered, un-
imaginable.

He felt himself, but unlonely and unafraid. He thought of
his body and the intense and unknown awareness of it when he

had been with Catherine. Lying with her had been the centre of the earth, a wild breath-taking thought, his being in a woman.

*

When Anthoni awoke the house was deadly silent; the sun shone obliquely through the window, just touching the wall. It was afternoon. He shuffled to the window and looked out over the street, he stared at himself in the mirror. He looked dreadful. There was an intentional slovenliness in his movements, a satisfaction in deciding that he looked pale and ugly. He sensed an immense power of restoration in himself, and was pleased with the idea of starting completely from the ground up. He liked the silent house in which he alone had been asleep; a feeling of indignation must have hung around his room; he looked at his clothes which were lying on top of his dresser. He felt very much a student, *die Freiheit zu verkommen,* Jaspers called it, the freedom to go to the devil.

He went down the sloping street to the corner where in a café the Dutch students had their club, which was called Hollandia. The upper floors consisted of rooms for rent, and in their better days the students had occupied almost all of them. Their money had paid for modernizing the place, and now that they were cut off from their families and lived on the meagre loans of the consulate, these rooms were too expensive for most of them. They still had their downstairs room which opened into the main one of the café, and there they used to eat and sit around.

Anthoni found it empty and sat down in a deep chair, he put his books in his lap and stared out of the big window into the rather sad little garden. It had an iron gate with an arch over it, and rows of crates along the house. The one tree shadowed it completely. He stretched, and went in to order the smaller of the two luncheons although he was very hungry. He tried to begin reading the introduction to a German book on electromagnetism from the university library, which he had dragged with him unopened for three weeks now. He thought: If I could think in rhythms, write poetry, oh I'd like to go under in a big messy city, a student in Paris in the Middle Ages, François Villon. He would borrow Villon from somebody, he wanted to write a letter, put in some lines from him, to Catherine.

The owner's name was Ernst, he was a small, stout man with a bent back who had been a sailor in his youth. Anthoni told him that a lady, a friend of his, wanted to stay overnight in the place, that was to say, could he reserve a room for her and what would it cost? Ernst was unexpectedly simple about it; he just said that there were several rooms free, and that they cost four francs for a night.

'Oh, that's not too bad,' Anthoni said.

He had read a chapter of his book when another man came in. It was already six.

'Toni,' he said, 'We don't see you much.' Anthoni could not stop himself from smiling vaguely and somewhat affectedly. There was a silence.

'I'm sort of working,' Anthoni felt compelled to say. 'How are you doing, Rolph?'

'I'm through till autumn. God, I hate the idea of spending another summer in this town.'

'Why don't you go somewhere?'

'There is nowhere to go here. I'd rather be in Holland.'

'What's there to go to in Holland?'

'When you're in Holland you can go to Switzerland in summer.'

They smiled and Anthoni said: 'I'm glad you are openly idiotic. Some of you people live in the most incredible vacuum. The damned thing is, it's contagious. I saw the Germans enter Amsterdam, if I ever would have thought that I would spend the year of the invasion discussing holidays in a Swiss café . . .'

'The invasion is postponed until next year.'

'Don't you want to go to England?'

'I'll be an engineer in a year,' Rolph said. 'Right now I am nothing, and no good to anybody.'

'You mean that you don't want to sacrifice your career. Jesus, if I remember well, you've wasted a lot of years on lesser things.'

'I don't mean that at all. This is a war of machines. When I'm an engineer I am a recognized organizer of machines. Nobody needs another infantry man.'

'The trouble is,' Anthoni said, 'that you're too right. A friend of mine, an American, is even righter. His point is that under the light of eternity one country isn't a hair better than another. I believe in not being right when right coincides in such an embarrassing way with your own interest. *Honnête homme vit contre son interêt.*'

'I'll have a drink. You too?'

'You're a wonderful man. Excuse me just a minute,' Anthoni said.

He went through the main room and into the telephone booth under the staircase. He had carried the twenty-centime coin loose in his pocket during the whole afternoon.

Catherine said in a light voice: 'Hello, this is Miss Valois.'

'Hello, Catherine, how are you?' Anthoni said. His heart beat very fast and he felt as if he had to make a public speech. I wonder, he thought, why do I do these things? The life of least resistance certainly has its attractions.

'I am fine, Toni, how are you? It is sweet of you to call me. Did you get home well?'

Those words surprised him, for her voice had sounded so noncommittal that he had thought she would never say anything to recall their night.

He asked whether he would see her during the week-end.

'I am sorry,' Catherine said, 'but that's impossible. I'll call you on Monday, or you call me '

'Monday, but that's four, three days. Oh my dear, why? Aren't you staying in town?'

'Yes I am,' Catherine said. 'I told you once I had other obligations, too. I can't change my life for you, Toni. I like you very much.'

'And tonight, can't I even see you tonight?' He hadn't really wanted that, he had wanted a slumming night. but in the happy thought of Catherine tomorrow

Catherine sounded as if she almost pitied him, very much understood him. She did not know that he was thinking of the week-end which now seemed endless and without content. She thought he wanted her, again, and more urgently

'I'll call you Monday morning then, please,' he ended lamely.

'Thanks a lot,' he said when he was handed a glass of Dutch gin.

'Tell me more about that living against your interest business. Isn't that contrary to a basic principle of nature?'

'It sure is,' Anthoni said. 'Do you feel like going to a movie and lending me the money for my ticket?'

'I can't tonight.'

*

The weather had broken and the lake was a grey sheet drawn with small circles from the rain falling down almost vertically through the warm air. Sunday, water rushing through the gutters, the streets empty. The shops were closed, the restaurants and the movie houses silent. In the big dining-room of the Baur-au-Lac one man was eating, neat and dry and showing that he had come to his table indoors, from his room, through the carpeted corridors, not seeing the sky. He had propped up his paper against his carafe and looked now at the endless Sunday-morning articles, then at the wall; a waiter leaned against the service door and stared into space. At Huguenin some ladies sat down at a window after the peeling off of clothes and waited for their tea to come, gazing at the puddles forming on the pavement of Bahnhof street. The Rex opened its wide hall for the first showing of a German operetta film with Marika Rökk and three out-of-town couples created a momentary queue; a man scrutinized the photographs and then put down his one franc ten, he left water stains on the carpet and the doorman took his stub without looking at him. The lights went out and the programme began. Not one separate cloud was discernible, the sky was a monocoloured ashen plate, there was a sigh in the air.

Late that Sunday afternoon in the unended rain Anthoni went along the Uto Quay, walking close to the houses, hurrying across at corners. It was darkening already, and the street lights were not on yet. He had left Day and his crowd who were going out for drinks and dinner, and he had declined the invitation to come along because that was far beyond his means. He went slowly, for it was too early to go eating at Hollandia. He wondered where Catherine was. Money seemed able to ban the melancholy from this day; a big room with many lights, a fire, music, people sitting all around, some on the floor, he walking in, saying a few words about a new play, a book. What play? The Zurich theatre was engaged in a hundred year old production of Schiller. But this was Paris; or even a post-war Zurich where one worked in order to have peace and isolation, flying to France for deep meetings with the world; to create a circle, write essays.

He turned a corner at Falken street and returned one block, back up Seefeld street, hastily passing Day's place again – they might come out just then. If he went on to Hollandia he would be an hour early, with nothing to do. If he went to the movie here he would be too late for dinner, but he could have bread and cheese then. A very uneconomical arrangement for it cost almost as much as the one-plate dinner. He should go to his room now first and read, work two hours. But there was so much to think about.

He had been to Geneva for his French contacts, Day had said, and there was some latent overemphasis in the way he said it; Anthoni felt that he wanted to impress him, seem superior in some way. He had refrained from asking anything about the results of that trip although it could have been of vital interest to him. He was not sure, but he thought that it was Catherine, his having been with her, which had made a change in Jean-Pierre's behaviour.

'How is your beautiful girl friend?' Day had asked.

Anthoni had smiled vaguely and said: 'By some miracle she is not yet sick of me.'

'Oh my friend see to it that she won't be. Just be the easily bored one yourself, don't be too eager. It's all very simple.'

'Yes, yes,' Anthoni had murmured without listening much further, thinking of these, the week-end days, during which his mind had slowly turned upon an image of her, slowly perceived how she had a lover, who visited her now, did they go out, did he stay with her overnight? He felt a fury in himself, which he averted in a gaudy projection of the wandering foreigner, the vagabond, stealing the love of somebody else's lady.

Day had made a gesture with his hand by which Anthoni's Catherine joined the ranks of a long list of big and small adventures which were amusing but should not be taken too seriously.

'Don't go away yet,' he had said. Soon afterwards some friends of Day had come with whom he would go out; one of them the girl with the Lorraine cross.

'Hello, Claude,' Day had said, 'remember my Dutch boy?' And he had enveloped them both in a smile.

'Of course,' she had answered. 'Charming that you're coming, too. We'll have a nice party.'

She was quite a dynamic girl, woman rather, it was inappropriate to call her a girl. She had dark and uninnocent eyes, she had cut her red hair. Anthoni had not said anything, not said that he wasn't going with them, nor much after that while everyone had been enthusiastically talking in French. When he had left he had not managed much more than a sort of bow in her direction, and had caught the surprised look which she had thrown at Jean-Pierre.

*

There was a deep fauteuil in the room of a clear yellow, it was the only good chair. Catherine let herself slide into it. Anthoni took a straight chair and sat on it sideways, folded his arms over the back and looked at her. 'I'm so happy that you want

41

to stay the night here,' he said. 'It seemed such a lovely idea. I hope you don't think it sort of grim here. Ernst is really a decent man.'

Catherine observed his face, his hands, then she said: 'I wanted this too. My rooms get on my nerves sometimes.'

It was an intimacy to undress in the same room with her, a cool intimacy in which she primly put her shoes next to each other at the end of the bed, and took off her dress, her underclothes, in an elegant, decisive manner, laid them on a chair, unconcerned because the idea of being concerned would never enter her mind, yet not at all as if she were alone. The room was not small and not unattractive, and she used whatever implements it had to offer in a natural way, the natural mastery of the rich over matter, he imagined. 'You are so astonishingly beautiful, Cath,' he said.

'I am sorry I hurt you,' Catherine said in the dark, 'I have a lover, and I could never break with him. Why should I ruin his life? He has done very much for me.'

'What has he done?' Anthoni asked tonelessly.

'I'll tell you about it if you want me to. I have known him since school. Before my operation. I was a fat girl then and I was shy and ugly. My sister used to ignore me in those days. She is five years older. He came to see me again after my return from England. I had taken rooms in Zurich and I was alone. I didn't know anybody well. During the week-ends I went to my parents in Shaffhausen. They are very unharmonious with each other. Hans really put me on my feet.'

'Is his name Hans?' Anthoni murmured.

'Yes. I wanted to paint. He may have thought that it was just the whim of a rich girl. That was what my parents said; he didn't say so, anyway. He helped me. He has a good eye. I worked like a fiend then. I have really always worked hard since,' she continued in a musing voice. 'I don't think one gets anywhere in painting without doing that.'

I have hardly ever talked with her about her painting, Anthoni thought, it must be so infinitely important to her, I should. Many shadowy ideas lived in him about art, painting, colour, a presumption of really knowing, or rather a faith in his ability to know if he wanted to, which was the same thing; telling himself: whenever I get to it. The mental effort to capture those ghosts seemed enormous, they slipped away, it was like trying to multiply two six-digit numbers in your mind. Discipline. He half-heard Catherine say something about Zug.

'Does he live in Zug?' he asked almost inaudibly.

'Yes. He is a civil engineer there. He only comes to Zurich on week-ends now. He knows that I'll never marry him. I can't give him much time, but I don't want to give him up. He is very good for me.'

'To you?'

'For me. But I do not need him any more. He needs me now.'

Is there such hardness in you? Anthoni thought.

*

They woke up almost at the same moment and he felt his mood, his heart, in an unstable balance, the hesitation between withdrawal and glorious acceptance, as he called it for himself.

He kissed Catherine, and then, very abruptly, he came to her. Suddenly he felt hot and sticky, his desire seemed to recede. He thought: frightening, I didn't know that could happen. He held her still, and moved himself, and then he could feel her again.

Afterwards he told her that there had been something wrong somewhere, and that it hadn't been his fault only.

'I am so sorry,' Catherine said. 'It is difficult for me, too, like this.' And she went on to tell him in her matter-of-fact voice that she preferred another way.

He was silent, then he asked: 'Why didn't you tell me before?'

'I didn't know it was that important to me,' Catherine said. The room was still. There was an impersonal excitement in its atmosphere.

He did as she had said and lay still behind her, feeling himself in an intense awareness, a sharp, a torturing, an exalting pain.

When they came out the sun was shining from high up into their eyes as they climbed the steep sidewalk to University street. The colours were sharp, there was a loud gaiety of red and blue around them. The day, the air, and the city itself seemed very young. He stood with Catherine at the streetcar stop, waiting with her; she did not want him to take her home. He saw a thin, frayed line of cloud far off to the west where the lake was. The stationery store had pots with cut flowers in a circle around the stack of the Zurich morning-papers. He took out a rose and stepped into the shadowy interior with it, 'Forty centimes,' the woman said. He came out and put it in Catherine's hand, she smiled without looking at him. Her streetcar came and she stepped in and sat down with her face towards him. Her eyes were very bright and she looked at him without making a movement as the car went around the corner and down towards town.

*

'I have to tell you about myself on this morning, Catherine,' he wrote her. 'I feel so light and so strong, I am going as in a dream. Dream formerly meant: mirth, did you know that? I am elevated and I have vanished.

'You know what Hegel in his philosophy calls *aufgehoben*? I don't think there is an English word for it. It is three things at the same time: lifted up, put away, and cancelled, not annihilated but taken in by antithesis and with that a new concept in which the old has lost its identity.'

He scratched out the sentence; it is too pompous he thought. She will think me ridiculous. *Aufgehoben.* '*Aufgehoben*,' he said aloud, 'what a strange word, that is what I am,' and he rewrote the idea. 'Oh Cath,' he continued, 'I hope so that you feel like this, too. I hope you are working today on this, on this upward feeling. It's the only thing I can give you, but I pray that you will accept it. I hope I may come over tomorrow and see you, I'll call you.' He scratched out the 'hope,' and wrote, 'please let me.'

'I like your portrait. You have been severe with your face, which is a very beautiful face.'

Later she thanked him for his note. 'I understood,' she added.

'Did you feel like that, Catherine, did you recognize the feeling?'

'Yes, I did,' she said.   *

Before Anthoni knocked on her door he had heard her voice, and he walked into the room in a frozen manner, having expected her to be alone, and he smiled diffidently at her and at a girl who was sitting opposite her at the small table which she had put in the middle of the room, parallel to the easel at the window and the couch at the door-side. He looked intensely at Catherine and formed with his lips a mute greeting of greater intimacy which did not reach her, while he felt the eyes of her visitor on him but did not look back. He was introduced and heard only her first name, Anne-Marie; she was a woman with a round face, a very feminine figure, almost heavy. She had a sleek black dress on and dark hair in waves around her head. He sat down on a hassock at the longer side of the table, between them, and leaned over and rested his head on his folded hands. He smiled around him, and there was a silence. He moved his shoulders back and looked aside at Catherine's portrait on the easel.

'Anne-Marie is going to sit for me,' Catherine said. 'We are beginning tomorrow.'

The girl said lightly: 'It's going to be heavy work, I think. Catherine must be an impatient artist.'

'Yes, I believe I am,' Catherine said. 'I'll scream if you change your position.'

'Is your portrait finished?' Anthoni asked, turning completely to her.

'Yes, don't you like it?'

45

Anthoni waited a moment before he answered with the sentence he had prepared, but the girl spoke before him. 'It's very good, Catherine,' she said.

'I think so too,' Anthoni followed. 'You have painted an aspect of you which I do not know.'

'Ha,' Catherine cried, 'it's harsh, I know... Every artist is ruthless, Toni. If you are not ruthless about your art you're an amateur.'

Anthoni made a vague sound and nobody answered. He felt a rising impatience with the situation, and got up from his seat, looked more closely at her portrait, then at another picture, then took up a book, opening it while turning his face towards the table, as if to indicate that he was still in their company.

When the girl left he pressed her hand with a smile and stepped over to the window. He turned around when Catherine closed the door and walked through the room to the table, where she put things on a tray and rang for the maid.

'I hope I wasn't unnice, Cath,' he said. 'I don't quite know what to say on these occasions.' Catherine smiled and said: 'You don't want more tea, do you? I can make you a drink.'

The maid left with the tray. He said no as her voice had made him think that she wanted him to.

'Art is ruthless,' he repeated questioningly. 'Would you sacrifice love to your painting?' he added in an abstract tone, looking ahead and then around at her.

'There could never be a conflict between the two in me,' Catherine said without hesitation. 'I can't live without a man, but I owe it to my work that it comes first. It's not egotism, it's my duty.'

He had made his question sound very supposititious, and not insincerely so; the words had formed in him automatically; it was the thing one asked a woman in a conversation of this sort, and it seemed as if after a few words she had begun considering her answer too much, too early. She changed her voice while speaking, it became light-hearted and with a twinge of irony. She could have answered anyone like that. There was

46

a warm politeness in her conversation, Anthoni thought, a pleasant thing, politeness is the saving grace in so many encounters of two ideas, two wills. Why did he want so very much to break through it, against his own realization and judgement? Why did he want her to say or do things which would make him suffer?

'Art –,' he said, and stopped. He made a step in her direction, and enclosed her face in his hands. Her expression changed completely. He kissed her. She pressed herself against him.

*

Plato, Aristotle, Newton, Hume, Descartes, Kant, the gilded letters said in the stone collar under the partly glass dome of the university hall; separately visible sunrays were entering through one pane, descending into the high hall, then suddenly vanishing in the same instant all along their length, intercepted by a cloud in the sky; voices murmured, scattered steps echoed through the marble corridor, somebody leaned over the stone balustrade and called down in a shouted whisper.

Standing still in the lobby, looking up at the drab-coloured glass cupola, Anthoni thought: learning, the only really important movement in life, the straight line of science, the old life was a closed circle, now it is a straight line. It breaks off at death, senseless, but it is continued by someone else. I would like to walk in these corridors with a man who shaped the world with his mind, by his words. An esoteric life, like a mandarin, the Academy; he saw himself walking along the grass paths on a clear morning, a hall, looking down upon the white houses of Athens. I just want to play with the thought, he said to himself, here in this filtered light of the lobby of the university I am a student, I create the settings, Greek Academy, a Paris turret with straw on the floor, the student of Prague writing revolution in Latin; but I do not seem to be able to make the mental effort any more. I make a schedule for later and sit down to stare at a stupid magazine or a double feature. It all seems so incredibly boring, these Swiss students busily making their little notes, busily talking and fussing about their papers and their exams two years and six weeks from now, all planned. The war, coming north through Italy, the small headline in the morning-paper : allied thousand-bomber raid, it sounds so odd, so normal in German; they ignore it, they walk off to their classes as if they had hired the world to fight for them and now sat down to bigger things. Out of the world, they think they are its umpires. I am going to the war, I have to go to the war soon, but how, I have probed every way. See the military attaché again? In the end it will probably be Day who'll get me out of here. I'll phone him and leave a message. Catherine – some vague perception floated before him, untranslated into words, in which he came to Zurich on leave, stepping out of an army car, their wedding, her father would give them a house on one of the Ticino lakes, he was gazing out over the azure water from his study.

He stood for a long time on the top step of the marble stairs which led from the entrance door of the university to the sidewalk of Rami street. It was still warm, almost sultry; the sun, appearing in intervals between the black and white clouds, low over the houses, stung. He sighed deeply, the strain of walking up the street, the few blocks to his room, to put his books away, seemed unsurmountable. The thought of his room with its little dresser filled him with aversion. He could come here earlier tomorrow, look at his notes before class. He turned back inside; in a little corridor which ended at a telephone booth stood two old desks. He put his books and his notebook in one of them, and feeling lighter, stepped quickly down the stairs, grinning at a girl who was coming up without looking at her long enough to see her reaction and become self-conscious, and almost ran down the street. He sang *Stardust* to himself, half aloud, stopping when a passer-by looked him in the face and taking it up again as soon as their heads had crossed, went to the other side of the street where he scanned the announcement of new plays at the door of the theatre without pausing, went across again along one of the narrow streets with little shops one after the other. He winked at an old man who stood in the doorway of a second-hand clothes store, and walked breathlessly into the Schifflande. He waved at Rolph and another Dutch student called Punt who were sitting at a table talking with their heads bent together, not looking very hard at him; then he sat down on a stool at the corner of the bar, against the wall.

When they later sat together it occurred to Anthoni, they are much older than I, eight, ten years, yet I feel the older one. No, I wouldn't want to be a student their way.

They talked about the fraternity of which the two had been members while studying in Holland. 'It seems archaic to me,' Anthoni said. 'I can see the point in hazing boys who are too full of high-school high spirits. What comes after that seems so not-of-the-times.'

'It would still do you a lot of good, Toni,' Rolph remarked with a smile.

'Yes? I don't want to learn how to be a clubman and one of the crowd. Isn't it sort of abnormal for men always to be together and drink beer and shout at waiters?'

'You are still at the age of running after women,' Rolph said.

'What age is that?'

'Toni is a good chap,' Rolph continued to the other man, 'but he hasn't learned the meaning of friendship yet '

'Why don't you find yourself a good friend, Toni?' Punt said.

'Oh, I've had some good friends,' Anthoni murmured with a slightly embarrassed defiance. I wish I could buy another Pernod, he thought. Three, I am at two ten now, the tip, two forty. He pondered, and added: 'I suppose I am not a man's man.'

'It's a man's world though.' Both looked at him with a certain sympathy. He felt as if he were being interrogated. He liked that feeling.

'I don't think that means anything,' he grumbled, 'a man's world. I don't think what it's all about is earning money or building bridges. How can you have understanding without the, the ultimate intimacy?'

'Love makes the world go around,' Thea suddenly said in a sober voice from behind the bar.

He looked at her, surprised. 'Yes, I believe that too,' he said softly.

*

One man declared that Pernod burns a hole in one's stomach when drunk regularly. Someone else stated that one shouldn't live regularly. A student named Wouter said: 'When I worked on my thesis, I drank a bottle of Pernod a night.' A bottle was too much, so nobody answered.

'It is an aesthetic drink,' Anthoni said. 'It is clear green like the sea, and when you add water it becomes pastel. It looks beautiful. In France they use only distilled water for it.'

'That's absinthe, I think,' Rolph said. 'I don't know whether it's the same.'

'Absinthe is worse. It's illegal here.'

Closing the door of the men's room behind you, and then leaning over in the porcelain glare, gazing at your face in the mirror. He made a grimace at himself, God, how white and drawn he looked, how different from what he had thought, he shouldn't talk so much, he was ridiculous. He put some water on his forehead, he felt strangely hot, half sick, what am I doing here? he thought. I should be at home, reading, invulnerable.

Out on the street he was alone all at once; he talked half aloud to himself in an unconscious playing of drunkenness, he walked with weird uneven steps, letting his hand glide along window sills, forbidding himself to breathe until his hand caught the next one. He heard a car climb the street behind him, it was an army truck. He felt exhausted and wondered whether to try for a lift; he made a gesture with his hand and thought it was going to stop, but it was only slowing down to go around the corner.

50

Unexpectedly he felt better, 'Bastards, Swiss bastards!' he shouted against the houses.

* •

The street had been completely quiet for a long time, then the silence was momentarily broken by hasty steps and laughter. It was Saturday night and almost midnight. Anthoni had his feet on the window sill, and half lying in his deep chair he was staring out, looking at the ribbon of dark sky over the dull rooftops of the houses opposite. He could not see the pavement, but he knew how the few lamps shone in the white cones of light on the corners. He had been hours sitting like this; he was so stiff that he could not move his legs and he felt too tired, too bored even for the effort of going to bed. There is somewhere some fire in me, he thought, if the bell would ring now, loud voices be heard on the staircase, friends coming to ask me on a wild adventure – God, I am a sad one, I'm thinking like the young hero in a Russian novel. What a waste, it has been such a beautiful day, but what was there to do? Saturday, my favourite once, coming home from school, or waking up late when it was vacation, the house all in a bustle, the maid washing dishes, the baker having a cup of coffee in the kitchen, a happy exciting day . . .

He had got up too late that morning for his class and had experienced an unusual irritation with himself at that discovery; then, thinking about the day, such a heaviness had fallen over him – Saturday, Sunday, a precious and never to be refound piece of time, he was young, the sun shone so brightly, and there was nothing, Catherine was out of his reach. A thin engineer from Zug had reserved her, chatting with her in Swiss-German, *wie gôts?*, looking at her possessingly – what did I do before her?, he thought, but that did not help, what then had changed so much? He felt impatient, unable to speak to people, to do things which had no connection with her. Nobody knew, and that suddenly seemed the worst of all.

51

He had not shaved, just brushed his hair back, and gone out to the Migros store at the corner of University street; he had bought bread and cheese on his coupons and a can of tomato paste; he had closed the door behind him and dumped everything on the table, decided not to leave his room nor show himself that day.

*

The wallpaper was a beige with zigzag lines which sadly looked as if drops of water were running down it. He traced one with his finger, he stretched his arms hard towards the ceiling and looked around him. The room was filled with that brilliant light that signifies early morning of a cloudless day. He felt dismayed; Sunday, why doesn't it rain, he thought. He put on shorts and a bathrobe and took his Electromagnetism. He was going to study on the roof.

When he came out of the bathroom his landlady accosted him. 'I have wanted to ask you for a long time, sir, but I see you so seldom,' she said, and paused as if expecting an explanation. He felt sure that she would come out with criticism of some sort and was ready to tell her that he didn't want to be bothered and was herewith giving notice that he was leaving on the first of the month. But it turned out that she was not going to speak about him, and he listened to a long story about a student who had left without paying, how she had retained his suitcase, how expensive everything was, that same man used a whole roll of toilet paper every week, she had kept track of it, and he had been from Holland too, and therefore she thought that he might know . . .

'I've never heard his name,' he murmured, 'but I'll ask.'

He climbed the ladder from the dusty attic, where there was a hard smell of sun on wood and where it was already hot, and came up on the zinc-covered roof, sat in his chair and looked out over the houses of Zurich sloping down towards the lake which remained invisible, and felt the soft dying wind strike over his skin. Just when he was thinking that an hour must have passed, the bells of the Liebfrauen church struck ten: he had been on the roof for twenty minutes. He squinted at the sun and thought, I'll sit here till it's straight over that chimney.

I do need some tan. I look sickly. The air vibrated over the metal sheets. Time was standing still.

Anthoni jumped up from his chair when the sun had almost traversed the obligatory course to the perpendicular of the chimney. He felt unable to sit there another minute, he was going to Ellis.

The Flora-street apartment of Robert and Ingeborg on a Sunday morning: the somewhat slight elegance of a low birch table, large couch covered with a vicuña rug, modern chairs; the blinds were drawn and patterns of sunlight swept slowly over the floor.

'The earth looks so lovely today,' he said, 'we have done such dreadful things with it, covered it with glaring dirty cities, oh, worse. It seems so incredible to me to open your eyes to the world on a sunny day in spring and know that you will have to get into a bomber with one chance in ten of being dead before the day is over – when you think about it, it's such an enormous act, destroying somebody, making his I stop, for ever more – don't you understand the Hindus who don't kill anything, not a flea?'

'Nature is nothing but killers and victims,' Robert said.

'Yes, but unknowingly,' Anthoni said in an undertone.

'Last winter I was caught in an avalanche on the Parsenn,' Robert answered. 'Did I ever tell you about it? At first I was in a panic, I tried to move my arms and legs and could not, as in a nightmare. Then I got very calm. I must have been lying there for two or three hours. It was late afternoon. I was completely certain that I was going to die. I worried about Ingeborg,' he continued with a smile in her direction. 'But about nothing else. It is not so terrible. You wouldn't want to live forever, would you?'

'Not in Zurich anyway,' Anthoni smiled. He felt a dizziness in himself, no not forever, of course not, but vanishing, not existing; he thought in a flash of Catherine. She had told him that she had very short moments, seconds, of consuming fear. His mind suddenly turned upon a friend he had had as a boy, who had seemed so strong and without doubt that it was as if nothing could go wrong on earth with him on it, and that death should not be dreaded since he was going to die too one day. He had met that man many years later and had remembered the assuring thought which then, on seeing him again, had become utterly strange and baseless.

'And yet you are going to be a soldier, Toni,' Ingeborg remarked.

'Oh, don't underestimate Anthoni,' Robert said. 'He can do his fighting in an office. And I think you would be a big fool not to,' he added gravely, looking Anthoni in the face. 'You want this war to be over, don't you? Well, do the most then that you are able to. Everybody can pull a trigger.'

'I'll be jealous of everyone who sits in a big chair in London or heaven knows where,' Anthoni replied hastily, 'I'll hate them, but I couldn't do the same. I will try to pull triggers. Oh, I don't think I'm brave. But once you are in it, part of your brain stops functioning. I have had that feeling before. I understand that I'm inconsistent. I would never have wanted to fight in any other war. But this time it's a true liberation, the saving of so many.'

'That's the devil at work,' Robert said, 'don't you know that through the ages he has made people think that just this once more, that on this one occasion, the end justified the means?'

Anthoni was silent. He thought of that office in London which he had just turned down, he was a staff lieutenant, driving along Whitehall in his jeep, a misty evening, a woman was sitting next to him with a cool hand on his arm; war, mutilation, and meeting Catherine again, one inch deciding your life, a bullet castrating you.

*

The non-progress of man, the dream of the march through the night; he was in a long file of feet, they were led under a stone

54

arch which was half shot away, and stopped in a courtyard. It was almost dawn, an electric bulb dangled from a wire spanned across the yard. An enormous German soldier, a Gefreiter, would start walking along the line, counting heavily and slowly: one, two, three, four, five, six, seven, eight, nine, ten. A frantic shock went along the line of prisoners, a muffled cry, a shiver of despair. The tenth man had sagged to his knees without a sound, a soldier who had been walking along with the corporal, behind the line, had shot him through the head with his revolver. The Gefreiter stepped over the man and went on: eleven, twelve. A wild fear seized him, he was already certain, he counted ahead of the German without moving his body: twenty-nine; he was thirty. He had known it before counting in a sickening revelation; he would be dead in ten seconds, it was impossible. He fainted and fell through space. The not-to-be-understood discrepancy, one man tightening his finger, and ending another, the thin layer of skin which separated life from eternal having-been. The burial preparations for the man who was still alive. He thought of the medieval fist fight in Valenciennes between two commoners, and the loser was hanged; and the revolutionaries who dug their own graves; so much more horrible the doctor, waiting in a chair at the gallows to take some gland fresh out of the body's head, it was for science, there you came between your guards, in the morning, always morning, and there was the doctor with his jar in which he would put the gland that he would cut out of your brain in one minute from now, mankind dooming itself. The soldiers of Westphalia putting a funnel in the throat of the farmer's daughter, they had all raped her, now they were going to fill her from the cesspool, it made them shiver and laugh at the same time, they liked that sensation; the Aztec priest tearing out hearts, kneeling over with one knee on the breast of his prey, kneeling over like a vulture, in furious haste, hundreds of captives, to go, the sun already past zenith.

The girl of thirteen who had haunted him, opening a law book at random he had come upon her case, in seventeenth-century England she had killed her mistress, and they had burned her. He saw her before him, a meagre little child, bound to the post in utter fright, the wood was lit, she was just weeping with pain, she must have been so finally and terribly alone, the earth to her such a deadly place.

The earth, covered with pain, with blood, with mangled bodies, I do it to you, I don't feel it. How can we ever expiate our sins, how can we ever erase our cruelty from time? He looked at the ceiling of his room and held his arms over each other, over his head, making the sign of a cross.

*

It was such a happy and comforting idea that it was Monday, a whole week ahead, work, shops open, the balsam of the days. I hate Sunday, he thought, and was on the verge of speaking those words when he checked himself. The week-end had not been mentioned between them, and Anthoni knew that he shouldn't although several times he had been on the point of doing so.

Catherine had said that she just had to see people, and so he had taken her to the Schifflande, his place; it was early and nobody was there that he knew. They sat down in the middle of the long side of the bar, Thea smiled at him and greeted Catherine very politely, and he half awaited in some uneasiness the arrival of the students who were almost always there at night.

They talked about the war and he said: 'Right now Day is my main hope. I've seen all the consuls and the ministers till we were thoroughly sick of each other.'

'Do you think Day really knows something about it?' Catherine asked.

'He has some good friends in the Maquis, and they are the people to get you through occupied France if they think you're worth their while. They have many lines and they have *passeurs* for the Spanish frontier. Trying it without a *passeur* and without contact addresses is completely hopeless, that's one thing I've learned.'

'What about the invasion?' Catherine said, and her voice

showed that she had all her knowledge on the issue from dinner conversation and that she never read a paper.

'What about it? I don't think it's true that they are going to wait another year. That's why I feel so bad about it all, I'd feel such a terrible fool if after all my waiting and running around I was still in Switzerland on the day of the armistice.' No, I couldn't have that, he suddenly thought, but I am talking a bit like a parrot, repeating my former self, do I really still want to leave Zurich so desperately?

'Will you wait for me to come back, Cath?' he asked, with a smile in which there was some irony at himself.

'Oh,' Catherine said, 'only if you return as a bigwig. I couldn't be seen with a soldier. I want you to come back in one of those tailored grey uniforms with a red and gold cap – or are they French? Oh, that bloody war,' she continued in a different tone of voice. 'You know, I think you should be careful. Day talks so much. I'm sure he tells you about his successes with women all the time?'

Anthoni laughed. 'I don't see him too often, but I guess he does.'

He told her about the waitress.

Catherine made a face. 'You know, Toni,' she said, 'perhaps the man is in love with you.'

'Are you, Cath?'

'No, really, there is something odd about him. He might be a fairy, and all his conquests are needed to prove something to himself or to the world. Well, anyway, he almost scares me. I know he doesn't like me,' she added after a pause.

'He is not at all a close friend of mine,' Anthoni said, 'but there is something amusing in him. And he is somehow very decent.'

'I'm not thinking of *Moral*,' Catherine said in German.

'I know that, clever girl. I'm not either. I do think it's a sickening business, in men that is. In women it seems poetic. It is different ... night in a Greek temple, the mystical orgies of Lesbos,' he said, all at once happy with those words which he knew would echo with her.

He was right; she smiled brightly, almost questioningly, at him. 'I tried to paint that once,' she answered, 'I will do it again later. It was too early for me that time. Have you read Bilitis, Toni? I'll lend it to you next time you come to my place.'

Later Rolph came in with Punt. Punt was more or less stranded in Zurich, he was well over thirty. He was very good friends with Thea, Anthoni knew; there was something nice and fresh about him and about all he did including that friendship. Anthoni did not know how intimate it was, but it certainly had not at all the colour of an affair between a flunked student and a barmaid. But then Thea seemed unlike any barmaid Anthoni had ever seen.

He introduced them, Rolph sat farthest away in the silent reserve which came over him on such occasions, Punt next to Anthoni. Punt was a very social sort of man, but there was an innate politeness in him which would not let him rule a conversation. They talked about Dutch gin which Catherine tried and did not like, and about the character differences between the French and German Swiss, and finally about Anthoni.

He felt very sure of himself, and there was a spark in him which showed in his words. Catherine wrinkled her nose when she laughed, and looked very sweet, he thought. He turned to Punt who knew what he thought just then and winked at him in an almost conspiratorial way, and who said aloud, without sounding wrong: 'What a fascinating girl, Toni,' and nodded, as if he now understood Anthoni better and revoked his words of last Friday in that same place.

'Thank you, Toni,' she said at her door, 'it was a very pleasant evening. It has done me enormous good. I needed to see some new people.'

'May I come with you, Catherine?' he asked. He found it difficult to speak. His mouth felt scorched. She hesitated a moment, then she nodded and went in ahead of him.

When he lay next to her he felt that she was wearing something under her nightgown. 'I'm not available tonight,' she said, with the corners of her mouth going up. He kissed her hair over her ear and lay still, on his back, turned his face towards her with a light smile; he had been afraid of making love to her, he suddenly thought. She bent over him and began to kiss him slowly and very deliberately.

'Careful, Cath,' he whispered later. He felt deeply shy, it seemed unthinkable to give himself that way, an unhappened ecstasy. She did not listen.

*

The box which Anthoni had brought with him into the auditorium and put at his feet during class contained a grey suit that had holes in the elbows and trousers with shiny knees. At the little shop in University street the Polish tailor had refused to try to repair it, and at eleven Anthoni went down the steep narrow street behind the university with it, scudding along with big deep steps into the old town.

The man to whom he showed the suit looked at him as if sure that there was a misunderstanding somewhere. 'It's all torn,' he said.

'That's why I want to sell it.'

The man put the suit back in the box and handed it to Anthoni. Next to his place was a pawnshop, but its owner stopped him from opening the box. 'I can't use old clothes,' he said.

Anthoni stepped out and looked at the window display with the box under his arm, waiting until some people standing in shop entrances would stop looking at him; he wiped his face and letting the box rest on his foot, combed his hair in the reflection of the glass. 'Damn it all,' he said. The best thing was to abandon the box somewhere, for the idea of carrying it back up to his room seemed impossible. He had only twenty-five centimes and the month had a week to go, nor did he know where to borrow anything. Taking Catherine to the Schifflande had been disastrous; he had vaguely expected that she would insist on paying for her own drinks, but she had obviously never dreamed that he would accept such a suggestion. For the first time his situation seemed to present an overwhelming handicap. He had told Catherine that he was without a penny like all Dutch students in Zurich, but she certainly could not guess how almost literally true that was right now. She had invited him to go to a cabaret with her that night, with her and a cousin of hers. Such a surprising and formal expedition; he had thought that it was because she wanted to do something in return after he had taken her out. The thing did not fit in their relationship which seemed based on an unspokenness, a status of dream suspended in time, a balloon floating through a wood; speaking, anchoring it, would mean its destruction. If she should introduce him to her cousin as if he were a casual acquaintance he would by the very act be reduced to that, he imagined, it was like forfeiting a privilege in the Middle Ages. A casual acquaintance, and very suddenly he thought of being in her mouth, of the night before, and he shuddered.

There was a disconcerting note about the rows of clothes in the windows of the many second-hand shops, they all looked completely new to him; how rich this country had become, the former picture of rocky lands, farmers scratching their furrows in a wearisome way, now it was so luxurious, a whiteness in the grey of occupied Europe.

He looked into an entrance and saw a middle-aged woman sitting in a chair on his side of the counter. She looked at him, and he stepped inside and took the suit out of its box. She turned her eyes on it, for a second only, and then she glanced at the one he was wearing.

'How much do you want for it?' she asked in what seemed to him complete irony. He stared over her head at the racks high up and made out a sign saying forty francs on a prosperous and fat-looking dark blue suit with black stripes. 'Five francs,' he said.

She appeared to take the affair seriously after all, he thought.

'One franc, sir,' she answered.

Anthoni was by now thinking in terms of weight only. Carrying out a piece of silver instead of the box which was coming loose all along one side was highly attractive. 'Two,' he said loudly.

She hoisted herself up, and he was just going to say, all right, madam, one, when she drew a register towards her. 'Sign here, please,' she asked.

Catherine was wearing a low-cut cocktail dress; she was standing with one elbow leaning on a bookshelf, looking with a frown at a man who was tinkering with the radiator. Anthoni had expected to find the cousin there and experienced an unforeseen joy. 'Hello, Catherine,' he said, and kissed her hand and touched her shoulder. 'I have had a day of frustration,' she answered with a half-laugh, 'for some reason they choose an afternoon in May to repair my radiator. We'd better leave anyway. I want to walk. My cousin will come to the theatre. I gave him the money for the tickets yesterday.'

'I should . . . ,' Anthoni began but did not finish the sentence.

'I hope you'll like it,' Catherine said, 'it is very good. It's Swiss-German, of course. Some things I can't follow myself.'

*

After the Cornichon cabaret he had muttered, what about a drink? feeling obliged to do so, and postponed pondering on the two francs of which one eighty were left in the pocket of his jacket. But Catherine had said that she was very tired, and they had both taken leave of her at her door. He had walked back to Parade Square in silence with the cousin who at the corner had said: 'I have to go left here,' in such a dismissing tone that Anthoni could not help saying: 'Well, good night then,' although he had to go left too; and cursing himself and the man, he had gone one block to the right, crossing Bahnhof street and almost running through a sidestreet back to the river, over the bridge, and not slowing his pace until he had made up for the detour and was on the quay, past the Town-hall Bridge he should have taken. It was only half past eleven, there were some people walking, some shop windows lighted. A cold wind was blowing that muffled all sounds except the river which was gurgling unseen in the dark. When he came to the funicular he heard the engine grinding; it was still running. He waited on the platform until the descending car came to a stop. It was empty. He sat down on the small wooden bench, an old man entered and sat opposite him with closed eyes, dimly lit shadows on his face. The car began jerking up the hillside.

He came out on the open space in the little park under one of the university buildings. He heard the fountain sprinkling and the wind wetted him when he passed it. He went out to the stone balustrade and looked at the lights below and at the sky. Some stars were discernible between the ragged masses of cloud which raced across. He buttoned his jacket and put up his collar, he stuck his hands in his pockets and stood very erect, inhaling deeply, with tears in his eyes from the wind. He tried to remember the lines which begin, this city doth for garment wear, he thought of an eighteenth-century etching, a lake with a murky moon, storm-swept waves, a boat dancing on it, his mind filled with images of night, he felt a wild and darkened beauty, all around him, in the world, the danger, the destiny of man.

He clenched his fist, imagining a dagger in it. He felt a small coin and took it out, spat on it, and muttered, oh Romans, Lords of the world, then he threw it out as far as he could. It flew wide from the slope under the balustrade and vanished soundlessly in the wind.

*

When Catherine came back into the room after having changed into a dressing-gown, he had taken *The Songs of Bilitis* from one of the shelves and sat down, he opened it and read a line aloud, and looked up at her. Her eyes were very light. 'Oh yes,' she said. 'It's not at all your style I'm afraid,

Toni. But you must tell me whether you discover beauty in it.'

'I was in love with Greece and Greek once,' he said.

'Can you read it?'

'I've forgotten about all, I guess. I can read the letters. And I still know *menin aeide teà*, that is, sing me of anger, my goddess,' he added, smiling at her.

'I am sorry that last night was not more of a success,' she said. 'I was very tired, I had been painting all day.'

'How are you getting along with her?'

'She has a very striking face. You can look at it.'

She stood up and turned the painting on the easel around. It was a sketch of Anne-Marie, with some colour filled in. She was lying on a couch in her black dress, her head on a dark red pillow. She seemed almost ugly; Anthoni remembered her face as much more regular. But there was a tremendous force in her features and in her body.

'What a beautiful and violent portrait,' he said, and he thought: God, she is a real painter, a real real one.

'She didn't make a move once in three hours,' Catherine said in an amused voice. 'I pay her for the sitting, you know. She works with a modiste, she doesn't make much money.'

'Where did you find her?'

'I've known her for a long time,' Catherine answered. 'She was once a friend of my cousin's, yesterday's, I mean. He has a very big crowd of people around him.'

Anthoni looked again at the painting. His dislike of the cousin had been instantaneous and deep, the idea that this heavy and strong woman should have been his friend, whatever that implied, was odd.

Catherine saw his expression and said, as if in answer: 'She is a Lesbian.'

'No, really,' Anthoni exclaimed. 'I would never have guessed. Did she tell you that?' he added, a bit shocked and not quite believing Catherine's observation.

'Yes, she did indeed,' Catherine said laughing. 'She wanted to go to bed with me.'

'Cath! What did you say?'

'I did. I wanted the experience, and she was so desperate.'

'But how could you, I mean what did you do ... ?' Anthoni murmured confusedly.

'She kissed me, but it left me cold. She cried for hours,' Catherine said and bent behind the easel and brought up a portfolio. She put a drawing in his hand of two nude women lying on a couch. It was very summarily done, the features were not worked out.

'She has a very exciting body,' she added. 'I mean from a painter's point of view.'

Anthoni gazed silently at the drawing and then got up and put it back in the portfolio with a sigh.

'And what with your cousin?' he asked, wondering while he spoke the words whether that was the wrong thing to say. Catherine might not have meant her remark at all like that.

But she had meant it that way. 'She wanted to try, but it didn't work. I don't think he was quite the man for an experiment like that. He is weak. What did you think of him?'

'He has a weak face,' Anthoni answered, 'at least that's how it seemed to me. He is uncannily like you, but in the strangest way. You have a very beautiful face, Catherine,' he added after a pause, when she had remained silent and had looked at him expecting him to continue. 'It's a very strong face too, I guess you knew that without me,' he went on, making a gesture at her self-portrait which she had hung on the wall. 'I don't know how he can be like you, he is, but without the soul, without the structure.' Why do I say all this, he thought, why so much fuss about this damned cousin? I just try to show how clever I am.

He wanted to add something quite different, to change the subject in an elegant way, but he could not think of anything. He frowned and looked at his feet.

Catherine enjoyed the topic. 'He is completely spoiled,' she said complacently, 'he has too much money, and he is not very bright, as you no doubt noticed. He is a celebrity, though. He has an enormous success with women, he has been to bed with everybody.'

Anthoni hemmed contemptuously. 'Women,' he muttered.

Catherine smiled at him. She hesitated. 'With me too,' she then said.

'You are crazy!' Anthoni shouted. 'No, Cath, it's not true.'

'Why not, Toni? Do you think that's wrong?'

'I only think it's disgusting. He looks so much like you. It's like making love with your brother,' he cried indignantly.

'It was four years ago, Toni,' she answered in a soothing voice. 'We were staying in Flims, where we have a summer house. I was just curious. He tried me later but I never let him again. He is not my type.'

Anthoni was silent.

'There was a grass field far behind the house,' Catherine continued in a light-hearted voice. "He used to go there to take sunbaths. He wanted to get a tan all over. One day I saw him lying there naked, his behind in the air. Since then he has always struck me as slightly ridiculous.'

Anthoni made a point of not smiling back at her. He was extremely vexed, he felt confused for many reasons not quite clear to himself. He could not now resist showing his annoyance. 'I am sure his tanned behind played a vital part in his Zurich successes,' he said with a cold, offending voice.

*

'Give me your dates once more, but exactly,' Day said sleepily. They were sitting out in front at a table on the edge of the café terrace, beyond the glass partition, where the wind could blow; early afternoon of a balmy day, the sun high over the quay, two old men leaning in the shadow of the one tree on the little square in front of them, girls in fluttering summer prints passing along the Limmat.

'December forty-one in Amsterdam,' Anthoni repeated. 'A friend of mine put me in touch with an organization that helped Dutch students get to England to join the army. I left with one address, of a man in Brussels. Shortly after the new year I was passed on to a photographer, near Monthermé, at the French-Belgian border. While I was waiting for the line to be cleared I worked with him. He had a group of four underground workers. Nothing sensational,' Anthoni added, to attenuate his words which had sounded too dramatic. 'Well, anyway, I was passed on into unoccupied France in August. The Vichy French arrested me, and so to Perpignan, work camp. Then after the allied invasion of North Africa the Germans took over there, too. A friend of mine in the town helped me escape to Switzerland. The Dutch here, the military attaché, told me to wait and just go on with my studies, they'd get me through. I'm still waiting. I've tried the English in Berne and the Argentines, and the Americans. I even tried the Germans, I never told you that one. But I never carried enough weight with any of them.'

He paused. 'The Germans?' Jean-Pierre asked.

'Oh, I had a try at a German visa to go by air, Zurich-Stuttgart-Lisbon, under a false name of course. It was such a beautiful plan,' Anthoni continued, getting enthusiastic again at the memory, 'going to England by way of a German airline – you know it's the only official transportation out of here. I had built up a tight case, address, police file, everything; I was a man born in the Dutch East Indies, under military age, sick with TB in a sanatorium here in Davos, and wanting to join relatives in Lisbon. I got a Dutch passport with a photo in which I wore enormous horn-rimmed glasses – I was completely invisible behind them – and as a reference on the visa application I had the nephew of the head of the visa bureau in Berlin. But the visa never came through. If they'd granted it, they would probably have arrested me in Stuttgart anyway, that's my one consolation . . .'

Jean-Pierre stared ahead with half-closed eyes.

'What a damned fool I have been,' Anthoni continued, speaking to himself, 'what an unforgivable fool. I missed my one chance. I should have gone south from Perpignan, to Spain. In those days, all that confusion, I would have got through, it was the only time...' He felt such an over-whelming regret that it seemed then impossible that what he was saying was really true, that he had made that mistake irrevocably, that no power on earth could redress it. The sensa-tion of the definiteness of it all filled him irresistibly. He pressed his lips. He had never suffered so acutely from this, he thought.

He had awakened that morning with a taste of failure, sud-denly he had imagined that there was not another second to lose. In a vague way it seemed the answer to everything: if he had only got through to England, he would be such a different man now. He did not bother to formulate that he would in that case never have met Catherine. He was not considering his life in actual concepts at that moment; he did not see himself in action as he once would have. A dim sense of missing fulfil-ment, the picture again of himself in uniform, driving into Tal street in his dust-covered army car. He had to do something right away, he had gone to Jean-Pierre's and waited for him, and brought him to the café. 'I have to speak to you,' he had said.

Day opened his mouth, and Anthoni interrupted him. 'I know, I know, no military training, not worth their risk and all that la-di-da. Listen, Jean-Pierre, you believe in the happy-few democracy, you do, don't you? Well, I am a friend of yours – just let me profit from that. Completely unjustified as it may be. I know about the rules. I don't care. I want to be an exception.'

Jean-Pierre had started smiling and his smile broadened during Anthoni's expostulation. He liked this. 'You are being a snob, Toni,' he said.

'Of course,' Anthoni cried, 'and I'm all for snob rule. Come on, Day, let's go, nepotism on the march.' He was very sharply aware of the fact that he had finally hit the right note. But I don't know whether it is for Day to decide the matter, he thought.

'All right, Anthoni. We'll try it. But don't expect too much, for it's not up to me alone,' Day said in a pleased voice which seemed to mean that prudence had made him add that.

'What do I do?' Anthoni asked.

'Write a letter and state you case. Don't hesitate to embellish the whole business as much as possible; they expect that anyway. And give references. You can put me in too. You can send it to me.'

Anthoni listened silently and began to wonder. A letter, he had written so many. Write a letter, he had heard that before. Oh well, why not? 'Shall I bring it to your house myself to save time?' he answered, 'I can do it today.'

'Don't bother. It won't make any difference. I'm not going anywhere till the end of next week.' The wind wrinkled the coffee in his cup. He tasted it. 'It's cold,' he said, 'Let's have another one. No, I have to go. Are you walking my way?' he asked, looking into the sun.

'No, I'll sit here a little longer,' Anthoni said.

After Day had left, Anthoni pushed his chair out of the way and stretched his legs, slumping down, then abruptly he straightened himself. He got out his pen and a leaf from a notebook, which he put in front of him. He started to draw a little star in the corner, avoided looking at the waitress who had come to take Day's cup away. He was going to write a letter to Catherine.

His change of mind and mood was a deep one; his confidence, inspiring what he had said to Day and inspired by that, had begun to fade. Perhaps he should accept the fact, he wondered, looking after Day who was vanishing in the silvery light with long strides, that there were no short cuts. If you wished to enter the allied world you had to fight your way out of this country and through the Germans, alone, unaided. He was seized by a fear, of one moment, that the time might come when he would have to do just that, knowing that it was impossible and deadly. Then he started thinking of Catherine again. Something was wrong.

Going to join the British army was, for him, not a brave deed. He had never dreamed of conceiving of it in that way. It was something he had to do for a number of undefined reasons, and for several childish and vain ones, which did not bother him because he was sure everybody who did a thing like that had them too and it was part of the game that no one ever spoke of them. Perhaps they were all that courage was made of. It was a dangerous thing to try, though, and those in Zurich who said they were not going because they did not want to disrupt their studies knew this and never questioned the motives for trying. Nor did the attachés and consuls he had sought out in Switzerland, in his vain attempt to get hold of a faked passport – the very fact that he wanted to run such risks was the unrefusable calling-card.

But now, today, something was added. Diminished rather. In his notion of failure of this morning was hidden the idea that he, somehow, had slightly spoiled his stand with Catherine, he had not understood quite why, and that the way out was a clear separation, while all was still well enough, starting anew later.

'I'm a coward,' he suddenly said aloud. 'I am afraid of living. If I spoil a relationship after three weeks, I would do the same again and again. I must just think better, analyse. It's time to grow up. She is so much stronger than I am.' He frowned, he pondered the idea of writing her a poem. It would be silly if it weren't very good, he thought.

'Sweet Catherine,' he wrote, 'I am sitting at a table of the Limmat-quay café in the sunny afternoon, and I am thinking of you. There is nothing but brightness in me now. It is the magic of your beauty. Know that I am always waiting to see you again, as soon as I have left you. I love you very much.'

Day's cup had left a circle of coffee on the table, he drew radii in it with the back of his pen until he ran out of liquid. He started to make a loop on the l of the word love, making it into a d. It did not look too messy. He wrote over love: desire.

*

He walked in front of her up the two flights of stairs and unlocked the door quietly. It was past eleven, the house almost still, a voice was heard from a far room without the words being distinguishable. He opened the first door on the left which was his room, and said: 'Please come in, Cath'; he locked it behind them and put the light on. In his unusually sharp glance, the room appeared small to him and rather poor, and he wiped away some crumbs which he saw on the dresser. He opened the window as high as possible and then faced her, standing with his back against it. 'Hello, dear,' he said. 'It's all right,' Catherine answered him in a reassuring voice.

'Don't you need the bathroom?' he asked.

'No.'

'Well, excuse me for a minute then,' he said, slipping past her with a shy smile, unlocking the door and closing it softly behind him, quickly crossing the silent corridor.

Entering, turning the key with his right hand behind his back, kneeling next to the bed and kissing her arm which was on the cover.

'It has been such a long time, Catherine,' he whispered, 'you must forgive me when I'm very quick.' 'Kiss me first,' she said softly. He looked at her eyes and then at her body, and there was an elation in him as he touched her.

Being so close to her, the unknown nearness, she offering her body to him, taking him, using him, a new and wild word, and the inexistent idea that he would be with her soon, that he was allowed to fall down the height.

*

His books were still in the little dusty desk where he had put them the week before. He took them out and sat down at a table in the university cafeteria with a pleased sigh. It was nine o'clock, he was going to be in time for his Saturday class, he had never quite made that, he felt fresh and everything did; the day spread so long ahead of him, with a happy richness of possibilities.

The man named Wouter came in and sat down next to him. 'Hello, Toni,' he said. 'I didn't know you frequented this university.'

Anthoni smiled at his ironical face. 'I don't need it as much as you. Lord, what a waste,' he suddenly continued, 'to lie in bed on a summer morning, to be unconscious. I am going to rise early from now on.'

'You once told me that that dulled the senses.'

'Yes, yes, but not today,' Anthoni answered distractedly. He didn't want to argue.

'I want some coffee,' Wouter said.

'Can you afford two? I'll buy you one next week.'

Wouter came back with the coffees and remarked: 'Not that I expect to see you here next week. These youthful spells of diligence don't last that long. I am going to stay in bed the rest of this week-end,' he went on, speaking more to himself.

'In that case you can certainly lend me something,' Anthoni answered, 'Thursday is the first of the month.' He smiled so brightly that it was clear he was thinking of something else. Cath, Cath, he said inwardly – the night was so much the present in him, he would not see her until next week but the week-end without her did not matter now, he wanted to run, to look the town in the face.

At eleven he took the streetcar down, he changed Wouter's five-franc note; it would be madness to spend it all before Thursday, he thought, starting to add debts and then dismissing them; he bought a paper and sat on a bench at the lake near Bellevue. Before twelve, the best time, the benches were empty but for one on which a woman with shopping-bags was resting, everybody was still at work, only tramps and gentlemen can sit here and gaze over the water; I want to be one or the other, never in between. This student poverty was not so bad, and all their complaining about it foolishness or hypocrisy. You signed an IOU which nobody, not even the consul, took very seriously and out you walked with your two hundred and twenty francs, big beautiful notes, hundred-franc-notes –

he might think of this time of waiting with regret later when he had money but no hours, was fitted into the make-a-living pattern, filling days with a routine to buy life for the evenings, the holidays, two weeks a year, having wonderful time. Unacceptable régime – he did believe in science, he liked it, but a day-long office, lab, no; I wish I could play the piano, play in a bar from ten till two in the morning, how attractive that seemed. To be an artist, marry a rich woman, he would be well able to handle money, he wouldn't squander it, he would not do nothing, he would work hard

He turned the pages of his paper over to the advertisements, his eyes went down the lost and found column. To find a wallet, open it, one hundred thousand francs, he would take a thousand-franc note and drop it again, no, he would certainly keep it, people like that were insured, then what? Go to a bank, put it in a safe-deposit box, pay for two years in advance, he could borrow money for that, he would not spend a centime, go on living just as he did now. After the war, come back and take it out, put it in a tobacco pouch, drop it in the crankcase of his car. In Paris he would buy gold with it, go to the Mediterranean –

The lake was smooth and glittering, he moved to the side of the bench where the sun was, sat on his paper and lifted his face to the light.

When the benches began to fill with children and young men with sandwiches in boxes, he got up, left his paper behind, and began to walk along the lake, looking the oncomers in the face and implying by his quick step that he had to go somewhere expectedly. He had a vague scheme that he should inaugurate this new day, this new life which he was going to lead, by a walk, a real hike following the shore, he should walk for at least two hours, get the lethargy out of himself, smell the sun, the water. But when he passed Flora street he happened to look up and see the name sign, and he began to hesitate.

It was an extraordinarily warm day, he thought, it was a bit silly to start a venture of that type on such a day. He dismissed that excuse, but then he realized how intensely boring it would be to come all the way back alone. It would be endless. No, he would not go now, but he promised himself to suggest this same idea to Goedkoop, a Hollandia man who liked those outdoors things. They might go together, tomorrow perhaps. So, crossing the road he went into Flora street and up to the corner where Robert Ellis lived.

Ellis was out and he sat in the window sill watching Ingeborg paste clippings in a scrapbook.

'Where has Robert gone?' he asked.

'He won't be back till five. I'm glad you came, will you keep me company until then?'

Anthoni visualized for a second the streets under the high sun. But where could he go from here anyway?

'There's an old film of Carol Reed in some dingy theatre somewhere,' Ingeborg said, 'which I have to see. You want to come?'

'Yes, of course,' he answered. 'Let's go now, then you'll be home before five.'

They got into a streetcar, and Ingeborg said: 'Robbie had to go to the library for his translation, his book on architecture.'

'Poor girl,' Anthoni replied, 'were you bored?'

'Yes, I think I was. What about you, Toni?'

'I'm never bored. Well, seldom. My theory used to be that only stupid people get bored. That's for men only,' he added. 'I'm afraid I'm getting more and more stupid,' he continued pensively, 'as a boy I used to read a book a day, and now when I'm in my room for more than half an hour I go crazy. It's partly the town, I assume. Don't you think so?'

Ingeborg looked at him. 'And where do you go in order not to get crazy?' she asked with a smile.

'What? Oh, to Hollandia, to a movie, or just down the road a piece, down to the sea in ships,' he murmured.

She glanced at him, she appeared to be wanting to question him on something but then thought better of it.

They had to change twice and came to an outer district where the car, all but empty, jangled along the rails with great speed, through deserted streets, men in shirtsleeves sitting on little balconies, snatches of radio heard at the stops, once a child's crying. The theatre was at the far end of Aussersihl, and in that sun-bathed street it was dark and uninviting. There were not more than four or five people. The film was called *The Stars Look Down*.

Going back their streetcar was so long in coming that they took another one, to Pelikan street; from there they walked to Parade Square. It was shortly before five and they walked quickly.

'Will you stay and have dinner with us?' Ingeborg asked.

Anthoni hesitated a moment. He would have liked to, he had planned to go to the Women's Club Restaurant which was cheap, nonalcoholic, and dreary, but something stopped him from accepting. He had an acute fear of overstaying anywhere, with anybody. 'No, thank you, dear, I really can't,' he answered, and was sorry he had said it the moment the words were spoken. On Ingeborg's face was an expression of regret. 'Oh damn you, Toni,' she said with half-joking irritation, 'you're always off to somewhere else.' Anthoni cocked his head and then cleared his throat self-consciously, thinking that he must look foolish. He bent his eyes on Ingeborg and thought, she seems somehow so un-, un- I don't know what. She has no sex appeal. For no particular reason he was seized by a sensation of pity. He took her hand and smiled at her. Yet she is a beautiful woman, his thoughts went on, she is so slender and blonde, she has a very fine and elegant face, the Zurichers certainly look at us. Suddenly his heart started to beat very fast. Around the corner lived Catherine. They were one block from her house. A feeling of panic caught him. He paled at the idea of meeting her, and he began to walk even faster, still holding Ingeborg's hand.

At the corner of Parade Square he slackened his pace. He cursed inwardly when he saw that their tram was just arriving at the stop. They ran to catch it. He was aware of sharp disappointment. All at once he had hoped to be seen by Catherine. He turned his head around before getting in but flinched when he gazed in the face of a man who was pushing up right behind him. The streetcar started moving, and Ingeborg gave him a light smile because they had just made it. He smiled back, and his heart was heavy. What had happened to his day?

*

On Monday morning as Jean-Pierre stepped out of the bank at the corner of Bahnhof street and Parade Square, he saw Claude. He did not feel at all like talking to her and was just slipping around the corner when she caught sight of him and hailed him. 'Hello, Jean-Pierre,' she cried. 'how well you look! You are bronzed.'

'*Hoehensonne,*' muttered Day in his heavy German, accentuating each syllable. He was referring to the sunlamp treatment which his barber had now persuaded him to undergo.

Claude did not listen to him. 'I'm always so glad to see you,' she rambled on in her Parisian French, 'take me for a cup of coffee, please. I know you've seen Pierre, and I want to hear about it.' Claude never left her room without pinning on a Lorraine cross, the emblem of the followers of De Gaulle, and she pursued the subject of Gaullism with a tenacity not quite in harmony with her person. There were several versions of the reason for her being in Switzerland, the wildest ones originating from herself, and some Frenchmen thought that she might be a German spy; but the truth was less exciting and she was probably just one of the French governesses caught by the war and somehow managing to avoid a return to the occupation.

She did not wait for Day who was thinking of a plausible excuse but took his arm and walked him to Huguenin, the tearoom.

'I am terribly nervous,' she said, 'I haven't slept for weeks. I listened to a speech of some colonel in London last night. He said to be ready for the invasion.'

Day remarked that that didn't seem so surprising to him.

'I don't know what to do,' Claude went on, 'I'm suffocating here. I'm going to Geneva tomorrow,' she added, 'I want to talk to Pierre. I might go to France.'

'Do you know him well?'

'Oh yes, we are good friends from the days I worked in Geneva,' Claude told him. 'How did he look? Was he optimistic?'

Day told her the story of Lennard's French enterprises without saying much that she couldn't have found in the *Neue Züricher Zeitung*. He became more animated while talking. He had had a very short-lived affair with Claude, but that was long ago. Their relation then had ended in catastrophe, Claude appeared to live without sleeping and had taken to morphine. But she was attractive in a very nice and French way.

They began to talk about the development of the war and Claude sketched the lines along which the invasion was going to proceed. She seems to spend her nights now listening to the radio, thought Day, who was basically uninterested in these armchair strategies and conceived of the war only as a cosmic struggle between civilized and beastly nations. He brought the conversation back to personalities by mentioning Anthoni.

'How do you like him, Claude?' he asked.

Claude considered the question and then shrugged her shoulders.

'He is quite amusing,' Day continued. 'He is a very keen fellow, you know. But too shy and too young. You are just the kind of woman he needs.'

'You told me that before,' Claude said. 'And never tell a woman that she is this kind or that kind. We don't like that.'

'I'm sorry he behaved so oddly that Sunday.' Day went on, unperturbed.

'What exactly are you up to, Jean-Pierre?' Claude interjected with a sudden sharpness.

'For heaven's sake,' Day protested, 'what do you mean, up to? I'm not a procurer, sweetheart. He was lonely at the time, and so ...' And he made a questioning gesture with his hand. 'He might moreover go to France, he wants to join the British army. It seemed a good idea to get you two together. But I guess time has moved on since then,' he added as to himself.

There was silence. Day said: 'If you are going to Geneva tomorrow, you might take his letter with you. It's for Pierre. I'm not going yet. Why don't we have some lunch, and then you can come with me to my house?'

Claude answered: 'I'm too nervous for anything of that sort right now. I have to arrange an affair of mine.'

Day did not ask what kind of affair.

After a pause, Claude went on: 'I have to borrow money somewhere. I'm without a penny, I don't even know yet how to buy my ticket tomorrow. I'll run around town today till I've found it.'

Day stared out of the window for a moment. A woman who was looking in at the cakes met the smile in his eyes and turned her head away. But he was smiling at himself. Then he shrugged.

'Let's have a nice luncheon, Claude,' he said. 'I'll help you.'

*

At six o'clock Day telephoned Anthoni's house. 'I want to leave a message,' he said. 'Just a minute,' the landlady replied, and then he heard Anthoni's voice. 'Toni, are you home? Come over to Mary's for a drink, say at seven. Can you make it?' 'Yes, all right,' Anthoni answered morosely. He went back to his room, he wanted to try and finish his chapter.

He decided to go by foot and plodded down the staircase in the steep street and to the small café in the old town which was called Mary's Old-Timers Bar. Day was already there, not alone as Anthoni had thought from his businesslike tone but in a large circle of people, and evidently in excellent spirits. The crowd was just breaking up and Anthoni was introduced to several men who shook his hand while waiting for their companions or looking for their change. When everybody had left, Day and he remained alone in the place. Day suddenly had a very different manner from a minute before. There was a tired warmth in his voice which pleased Anthoni. It was as if Day knew that he could be himself now, without any bar gaiety or cynicism.

'How damned superficial everything is, Anthoni,' he said.

Anthoni smiled at him.

'I know that you think otherwise,' Day continued in a wistful voice, 'I envy you sometimes.'

'You are almost hopelessly spoiled, Jean-Pierre,' Anthoni remarked.

Day made a bored face. 'Come on, Toni, that's not the secret. As soon as you are back in the money you'll do the same things I do.'

'I certainly won't,' Anthoni answered, 'for the very good reason that you don't enjoy yourself.'

'Don't you enjoy a good dinner?'

'A good dinner,' Anthoni repeated with the utmost contempt he could put into his voice. 'For God's sake, Jean-Pierre, you can do better than that, are you completely insane?'

'Go on,' Day cried, 'I feel better already.'

'I'm not playing the ascetic,' Anthoni said, 'I'm on the verge of robbing the Swiss National Bank, but this good living of yours isn't immoral or anything, it's just so very uninspired and insipid . . . I think,' he added after a slight pause.

He went on with his favourite hyperbole. 'Life, twentieth-century life is a straight line. It used to be a circle.'

Day regarded Anthoni expectantly.

'I mean,' Anthoni said, 'that life for, say, a Babylonian peasant – or for one living now – that life for those people is a circle; they live like everybody around them, before them, and after them. The only milestones in their lives are birth, marrying, children, death. And they die when the circle is completed, tired of their days – when they are lucky, that is.

'Modern man,' he continued, preventing Day from interrupting by a wave of his hand, 'lives in a straight line. As soon as he becomes conscious of himself he starts striving for something, and he never stops. When death hits him, he is just thinking of a new concept or a new house or a new mistress.'

The mistress he put in to provide some French colour. Day looked at him with a pleased grin, like someone who has gone to see his favourite boxer and is not disappointed. 'You're a highbrow,' he said. 'I like it, it's a nice change. Not that I see your point.'

'Oh, I don't know,' Anthoni replied, 'I guess I want to say that you have to adopt the straight line. Unless you are content to live like a hermit or like a cow. You are meant to go somewhere.'

Day assumed a sober aspect. 'There is no place for men like me in that scheme of yours,' he remarked. 'Too much thinking tires me.'

'Oh come on now, Jean-Pierre,' Anthoni almost shouted, 'you know as well as I that there is some fundamental decency in you.'

'Thank you, my friend.'

'Of coure there is,' Anthoni said convincingly. 'If there weren't you'd be making millions right now in Paris with black market grain. So be yourself,' he ended rather anti-climactically, in a trailing-off voice.

'Are you in love, Anthoni?' Day asked.

Anthoni reddened. 'No, I'm not,' he answered in a tone which struck him as being defensive. Why on earth was it?

'Be sure you don't convince yourself you are. You should marry the girl. But that is quite a different matter '

'Is it?'

'Of course. That's one thing you should learn from a Frenchman,' Day said somewhat coyly. 'Marriage is an affair of business. When people say that they love each other they mean that they want to make love. You don't have to marry for that. If you do – so much the worse. After that phase is over and done with, you'll find that you have nothing left.'

'Not very original, and you are playing with words. Love making is love making. It is very unidentical with love.'

'You are in love with her, then.'

Anthoni shook his head with a laugh. 'I don't believe in love on first, or second sight.'

'Marry her, Toni,' Day said pensively. 'Be careful not to fall in love with her, but marry her. That is the best advice anyone could give you.'

Anthoni made a grimace for an answer, and then he asked: 'What about the wars, Jean-Pierre?'

'Hurrah, the war,' Day cried at once, 'yes, that's why I phoned you in the first place. Your letter is on its way. I'll explain to you how your case stands.'

Love ... I want to be lifted by it, love is not an inspiration, love is volition, Anthoni thought.

*

Anthoni walked home through Tal street, hesitating for only one moment when he passed Catherine's door. He was on the other side of the street, his eyes went up and rested on the lighted windows, her apartment was on the back side, he wondered whether she was home. She had said, I'll phone you, Monday, and he had decided to stick to that, and not be the first one, and he had waited the whole day for her call. Now he actually saw himself crossing the street, pushing the bell, no, that he could not do. He pursued his way, two more blocks. He entered a telephone booth.

Leaning against its wall, putting his feet up on the ridge on the other side, reading the instructions black on yellow in four languages. What casual words could he say; she wasn't at home probably, he grumbled, and therewith stopped his reflections.

'Hello, Cath,' he said, 'how are you? I just wanted to hear your voice, and I wanted to ask you for the theatre, on Thursday, the first – do you want to go with me? No, I'm not at home, I'm in town.' He sounded irresolute. 'Yes, I'd love to come over.'

Later that evening he suddenly asked her: 'Have I disappointed you, Cath?' She looked pensively at him.

'I thought, I thought,' he said, feeling that he was blushing, 'I remembered one of our first times together ... It was a

80

Sunday,' he added almost inaudibly. 'I mean that perhaps, if I had been a different man, you might have decided not to see your, that engineer again.' He had hoped for a denial, explanation of that one Sunday – Catherine did not answer, frowning fleetingly, then seeming to be lost in thought.

Anthoni was now regretting that he had uttered these words. 'You know, Catherine,' he said, his fear of being ridiculous and weak making him speak in an ironic tone, 'I'm in a very transitory state – I'll be a new man one of these days.'

'I wonder whether I am good for you, Toni,' Catherine replied.

Good for me. A new formula, no, you are certainly very bad for me, he thought. He looked around the room, for a moment he had the terrible feeling that he had spoken those words aloud, that she must have heard them, read them on his face.

'Yes, you're good for me, Cath,' he said.

He woke up in the middle of the night and tried to dress in the dark, stumbling, almost falling while putting on a shoe, in a half-dream, the walls swaying, lights and voices in his head. He sat on the floor to put on the other shoe, he felt utterly and bottomlessly spent, exhausted as never before in his life, what has happened to me, he thought. He felt a hatred almost of Catherine, man must create, I cannot live up to my 'equal rights of man and woman'; that is why people go to whores, he thought, not because they cannot find anybody else, a brothel is a bulwark of culture, to clear yourself to clear your being, clear the decks, for thinking, working; to make love happily and instantly and then thank your girl and out into the air, no pretence, no simulating of new desire, no waiting, no apology, no feeling of guilt for being alone in having it.

He stumbled to his feet and shook himself like a wet dog, he kissed the tips of his fingers and touched her hand with them, she had fallen asleep again, and went down the stairs, with closed eyes, counting the steps, opening his eyes on the thirteenth, out into the street.

*

Catherine was going to buy a new phonograph and he was coming with her, supposedly to give advice although he was aware that the chapters on the electromagnetic field which he had read by now did not help any in a radio shop

She sat down on a chair at the counter and he stood next to her, looking out of the window and then reading a list of new recordings on the wall.

'I want a phonograph,' Catherine told the salesman, and added, 'I think I should buy a new radio too. Do you have Marathons?'

Anthoni was surprised and amused that she obviously knew so very well what she wanted without any advice, and by the smooth way in which Catherine decided to buy a radio; in his present frame of mind such easy spending seemed romantically bold.

Catherine turned towards him. 'They are made in Vienna,' she said, 'and it is the best thing there is right now. My mother told me about them.'

A grey radio was brought, in a metal casing, which had a very efficient and expensive look. Catherine nodded and bought an automatic record-player with it. 'I want them delivered, please,' she asked, and added to Anthoni, 'You'll read the instructions and show me, won't you?'

The salesman grinned at Anthoni with the conspiring smile of the technical-minded male, but Anthoni pretended not to notice him.

'There wasn't much to this expedition,' he said in the street.

'I'm glad I have them,' Catherine answered. 'It's a belated birthday present from my father.'

'I'm so grateful for your trouble, Toni,' she told him back in her room, 'I do have to work now, but I'd like very much to see you later. Perhaps you want to come for a drink if it is not too far out of your way again?'

He shook his head for an answer. 'Yes, I have to go to the university too now,' he said. 'I'll be back around five.' He kissed her on her cheek; when he left the room she stood pensively in front of her easel, and hearing him opening the door, she moved her face towards him and smiled.

At five, coming to her floor, he saw the door standing open, her room was empty and he stepped in and walked over to the window to look at the painting of Anne-Marie. She had worked very hard, he reflected that he had liked it better in its sketched stage, the colours seemed so full, too complete, filling their extent in a hard, unmodified way; but regarding it longer that unqualified colourization gained an unexpected momentum, it had an aspect of Modigliani, where was she going, it must be all but impossible to follow a course of your own amidst the violent currents tugging on all sides. He would say something about that to her.

Catherine came in from the bathroom across the hall, her hair up, in her dressing-gown. 'Hello, Catherine,' he greeted her, 'how lovely and fresh you look' He was getting up, but Catherine had vanished already into her bedroom. 'Ten minutes,' she said, and left the door ajar.

'Can I talk to you while you dress?'

'Please do. I finished the portrait.'

'I saw that. You must have worked like a beaver.'

'Yes, I did work like a beaver,' Catherine repeated in a pleased voice, the pitch going up towards the end of the sentence, her half-amazed way of speaking when she considered something slightly comical or otherwise out of the frame of what must have been established in her mind as standard Swiss vocabulary.

'I like it,' Anthoni said. She was rustling with a dress, she had not heard him, and he shouted: 'I like it. Cath!'

'Good,' Catherine shouted back in a muffled voice.

'I thought of Modigliani.' Catherine made a discontented sound. 'How do you avoid being swept hither and thither by all those painters?' he asked.

'I never look at them. I never open an art book any more. I only study the old ones.'

Catherine came out of the bedroom in a dark blue dress, carrying a book, holding out her hand to be kissed. 'I have to go to a dinner tonight,' she said, continuing, 'I told them I might bring a friend along. I hope you will accompany me?' Anthoni had uttered a silent damn when she said that she was going out to dinner, but when he heard that he was invited too, he realized that he would rather have been in the sulking position of the left-behind than facing the task of being not undistinguished compared to others in Catherine's eyes.

Catherine showed him the book. 'Anne-Marie brought it, I asked her to get it for me.'

It was a volume of Greek verse, beginning with Sappho, the Greek printed on the left-hand pages, English on the right. 'I want you to read it to me,' she said. 'When we are back home tonight.'

*

Their host still had a car at his disposal, which he sent for Catherine. 'He is a director of Brown-Boveri,' she informed Anthoni.

'Is he a friend of your father?'

'I met him at my parents', but they seldom see each other now. My father has an affiliated company, and he is more or less independent of the main firm.'

The house was far out and high up on the eastern shore of the lake. I wonder exactly what I'm doing here, Anthoni thought, standing at the window of the marble-floored room into which they had been led. There was a wood fire burning. Below him and distantly in the pale evening were the two rows of light from each bank, converging like a V into the bright knot that was Zurich. He looked at Catherine without knowing what to say. The surroundings were so oppressively rich, and he felt defiant, seeing himself at dinner speaking on war, on capitalism. I'm not a boor, I will shock them in a refined way, I won't be one of those people in an English society novel who talks about Marxism while eating the fish with his spoon and ends up by falling in love with the daughter of the earl. I can meet them on their own ground, but I know more than they and I like the world which to them seems so inimical and forever bent on their undoing.

But the host was a youngish man with a serious face and a serious suit who kissed Catherine's hand and took no trouble to find out Anthoni's name which he had obviously not caught. There were two others, a young woman and an older lady, they all knew Catherine and they greeted each other politely; their relation to the host was not explained. Anthoni had been afraid of the usual questions about Holland, his family, his plans, but he was annoyed when it turned out that he would escape these entirely; he floundered between an icy isolation and the desire to please and impress these people whom he saw as unshakably sure of themselves. He felt that nothing he could say or do could exasperate them or penetrate their placidity. How wrong I was, he said to himself, my host wouldn't raise an eyebrow if I were to tell him that I was a desperate anarchist. He'd gaze at me as he gazes at the headline about a train accident; the unpleasant things in life, one knows that they are there without having the time to worry about them right now. He'd probably telephone the police about me, though – just a routine obligation of his Swiss citizenship. No, he wouldn't, he would think, oh well, since Catherine Valois sees something in the young man ... Why is my presence taken for granted in such an uninterested way? Do they know that I am Catherine's lover? One of her lovers, he whispered slowly to himself. Is that one of those things one doesn't inquire after in this hard and wealthy world, in which each and every person does exactly as he and she pleases?

I'm glad I don't dine like this every night, too much food, butter, cream, wine, it's stultifying. I am half asleep. It is strange how nothing on earth could have given me entrance to this room but a woman – there is something exciting in that.

He felt Catherine's eyes on him and he looked back. She smiled. She is very bored and very beautiful, he reflected. She is self-conscious with people, how strange, she is not sure of herself. He returned to his former trend of thought.

It is one of the rules, a man can insist on seeing a woman, no matter how endlessly, he can follow her like a dog, make a fool of himself, still it is done in her honour and it does not lessen him. Insisting on anything else in society is bad form, imagine me telephoning this man, asking him if I could please come to his dinner.

Is that a real Renoir? I think it is a very sad one. It's an investment of course. They might as well hang their bonds on the wall.

He was going to say something about the Renoir, but just then the dinner broke up and coffee and liqueurs were announced in the adjacent room.

*

For some reason he knew that he should not talk about the dinner, it was on his tongue to ask who the two women had been, and he thought, oh hell, small talk, it cheapens, I could not care less. Why this Greek book?, his mind went on, it's intriguing, Cath wants to heighten my stature even if I do not take care of that myself, she asked me about my Greek and then got the book, what a very special thing to do. A yet unexperienced feeling of tenderness towards her rose up in him and left him all warm, and there was an illogical compassion in it, as if, he thought, her hardness were self-protection, her egotistic world the only one in which she could survive, and nothing more cruel than to try and make a breach in the walls. Vaguely, he formulated the idea: 'I must try and play my role.' Just for that one moment his path appeared so very clearly before him, and he saw how to give love to her, how it was right to pledge that to himself, he would begin loving her through it, and be loved. He wanted to put this into words for himself, but then a new confusion arose. Why was it so contradictory: to play his role, serve her picture of the world, not unravel it, and on the other hand be stronger, be a better man than he was now, dominate instead of ask? He would have to reason this out, alone.

'Come on, read,' Catherine said in the voice of a child, sitting on a pillow at his feet. As soon as he had come in she had put the book of Sappho in his hand.

He read out the Greek, without having time to think about the meter or glance at the translation on the right-hand page. He recognized only a few words here and there, but he consciously tried to speak poetically, looking down on Catherine's face at the end of each verse. There was a pleasure in this, and a dim regret; why had he forgotten it all, he should buy Homer, one of those paperback translations, begin rereading it.

He stopped after two pages. the literary thrill Catherine could derive from this must be limited, he thought.

'Do you understand it all?' she asked.

'Not a word.' But when he saw that this was the wrong thing to say, that it was inconsistent with being able to read the hieroglyphical letters and with the spirit in which she had asked him to do it, he continued: 'Not very much, anyway.'

'I want you to read some more to me in bed, later,' she answered.

Anthoni repeated to himself, in bed; these words should not be heard by him without a visible reaction, a woman telling him in those few words that she was willing and prepared to make love to him, to him, that very evening, as soon as he chose to. He smiled hesitantly at her.

'The son of James Joyce lives in Zurich,' Catherine said to him. 'Joyce himself lived here too, you know. I met the son once, somewhere. He had a good education, he speaks beautiful French. But he doesn't produce anything. I think he is the degenerate generation. Everything must have been spent in Joyce himself.'

'What a romantic conception,' Anthoni replied. 'I don't think the genetics people would accept it, though,' he added as a casual thought.

But Catherine regarded him, very surprised.

Anthoni felt obliged to go on. 'You couldn't write that idea out in a law of heredity.'

'Of course you could, and even if you can't does that make

it untrue?' Catherine asked, as if convinced of the absurdity of an affirmative answer.

'Yes, it does,' Anthoni said too loudly. 'A thing which cannot be formulated does not exist in science. That is why matter and even time are discontinuous. An infinitely short piece of time has no meaning only because it cannot be registered.'

Catherine answered his tone of voice, she hadn't listened to his not very consistent words. 'You are studying physics,' she said almost scornfully, 'you must have heard of the fourth dimension.'

'The fourth dimension,' Anthoni began, but he checked the impatience in his voice, and went on more calmly, 'the fourth dimension has no meaning in reality, dear Catherine. That's one of those dreadful popularizations for the Sunday paper. It is only a mathematical symbol.'

*

She had told him that he could come the next evening, late, if he wished to see her. It was the first of June going to the theatre had not been mentioned again, and he had brought her a present, Joyce's *Dubliners*, which had not been on her shelf. 'This is my favourite of all his books,' he said with a nervous smile. 'I do admire him, you know.'

She was very pleased. 'I love presents,' she stated. 'It's very late but you must hear my phonograph.' She put on a song which went: 'I never knew the technique of kissing. I never knew the thrill I could get from a touch, never knew much, oh look at me now, Cleopatra . . .'

Anthoni laughed. 'It's a sweet song,' Catherine protested, 'it's my favourite. Do you love jazz? I do, it revitalizes me in an incredible way. I would get off my deathbed if they played jazz for me.'

'You are a very special creature, Catherine.'

Catherine never avoided herself as a subject. 'Why?' she asked happily.

'Oh, I don't know, most women would be sort of apologetic about Cleopatra' – he pointed at her record – 'would consider it unworthy of their artistic niveau and all that; you're a vessel of contradictions.'

'Isn't that exciting?' she answered, and taking him by his hand she went into the other room.

There was such a gay simplicity in her that evening, he thought, and he felt strong through that, he held her hard and she asked brightly: 'I am very close, you? Can you be with me?' and he was.

'You must now stroke my back,' she said later, 'my mother used to do that sometimes until I fell asleep. And tell me a story.'

'I don't know any,' Anthoni answered. 'Yes, I do.' To his own amazement almost he began to tell a story.

It was about the man who goes somewhere by train, he picks up a newspaper from the seat and while reading it a strange sensation creeps over him, he looks at the dateline, it is tomorrow's paper. He makes a fortune that day by referring to the racing results and placing every bet right, but at night, alone in his hotel, he suddenly sees in that paper his own death announcement. 'And in the terror that seized him, his heart stopped beating, and he was dead,' Anthoni said. He had, and he knew this, never told a story so well. For while telling it a strange wholly uncalled-for terror had taken hold of him, and he spoke about tomorrow's paper with that fear in his voice, and he was frightened most by the weird entrance of fear into that quiet and so very unlonely room. He was glad when he was done.

Catherine shivered happily and turned around to look at him with appreciation. 'You tell beautiful stories,' she murmured, and closed her eyes and fell asleep. He reached over her head to put out the light, and lay in the dark staring at the ceiling; he was going to master his thoughts. Then he fell asleep too.

*

The dinner of the Brown-Boveri man made a good tale for his Sunday visit to Ellis.

'The Swiss plutocracy is highly interesting,' Tllis aid. 'I don't think you'd find a comparable institution anywhere else in the world. You know, it doesn't shape Swiss society and it doesn't make them any less gloatingly democratic. It is like their Edelweiss, it grows only on the highest peaks. It's nice if you can get at it, though.'

Anthoni smiled, he could not help being slightly flattered by the surprise he had caused telling them, rather vaguely, about that evening. In the light of such a reception, the evening started changing colour for him too. He knew that during the endless eating he had been unhappy, bored, and rebellious in turn and had only waited for it to be all over, and he was astonished at his own feeling now, a slight regret that he had not harvested more impressions, and then, a sense of having visited one of the sights of the world, an experience which he could now safely store.

He thought, my pleasure is entirely that of having done, and that is not all, it is a pleasure derived only from the reaction of others, of Ellis and Ingeborg. Am I a tourist in life, visiting the museums only to make check-marks in my guide-book and write home about them? I have a vicarious soul. A vicarious soul, he said to himself, I used to feel so keenly, where has my acuteness gone to? Perhaps we do not feel after our eighteenth year, our hearts petrify, like our bones, and we live on reflexes, a film settles over our senses and nothing penetrates anymore; one day you are old, your life is over, and you look around and say, who am I, who is that stranger, my wife, what has happened to that unique and unredeemable gift, my years – oh, he thought, I want to break through, I want to love; I do not want to be, to be with Catherine in that way which might be labelled: 'if they could see me now . . .'

'Money,' Ellis said, 'is a medium which buys you enjoyment as an individual, but in essence it is a medium of society. It certainly has as one of its main functions to distinguish the man who has it from the man who hasn't.'

'Robbie, this is not one of your translations, you are not

paid by the word here,' Ingeborg said. 'Can't you be more to the point? Toni has fallen asleep long ago.'

'I am right on my point now' Robert continued. 'The point is that only in this little country is wealth not used as a mark of social distinction. When a Basel businessman buys his wife a mink coat, she puts it into cold storage immediately. In every other place in the world people try, consciously or not, to arouse the envy of their neighbours. Here they are mortally afraid of doing so.'

Anthoni had listened to this, and he said: 'My host, though, had no qualms at all about parading his possessions.'

'No, you are wrong there. You slipped through by mistake. It's such a nice point,' Ellis added, getting enthusiastic about his own ideas, 'an aristocrat of the old school wouldn't invite, say, his bookkeeper to his table because he would consider him not his equal. The Swiss equivalent of a baron doesn't because he is afraid of the man's envy.'

'Ha,' said Anthoni, 'this will be the last country of them all then to hold off the revolution.'

'Yes, quite right,' Robert told them, 'and don't be too snooty about it. One day we'll be happy to sit it out here.'

Anthoni knew that he had to object to this, and he forced himself to keep his thoughts on the subject.

'You are as wrong as can be, Robert,' he exclaimed, 'you know where you can avoid that revolution? In England, where right now no man can have a dinner that costs more than five shillings, no matter who or where.'

Robert smiled. 'You are an indestructible Anglophile, Toni.'

Anthoni laughed, he liked to be called that.

'Listen,' Robert went on, 'I am as grateful as you that Germany is losing this war. But I don't think that it is in principle being fought for any reason but the permanent one for England, that is, no big power on the Continent.'

'Please don't tell me that Hitler is the Napoleon of our day,' Anthoni cried.

'The only difference is the difference in time,' Ellis replied.
'Well, let's say the main difference.'

'Robert, you know better than that. Not a million years could give any romance to Hitler. But Napoleon was a different man – at least until he finally went mad too. He didn't try to reinstall the Middle Ages, he ended them. He defrosted Europe.'

'But I liked the Middle Ages,' Ellis said pensively.

*

How infinitely wide the earth once was, boundless and dark; travelling, moving slowly through the land and through the sea, not a being sped along in the vacuum of a machine. It was such a short time ago only, a French officer riding from Vienna to Paris; in his days for the first time, his were the first days since the beginning of the world that it had changed, it seemed such ill luck. He thought of a room, he dimly recalled the high window, the stacks of books on one side, his grandfather's library, on the table a magazine, he remembered it Italian – but how could that be? – on its cover a panther attacking a man riding a camel; and then the books, the encyclopedia, and the atlas with the many white spaces. A part of the world was left white, and it seemed to him as if any white space anywhere in the world would make the world different, another kind of place and as if with the vanishing of the last never-seen land a glory had gone out of living forever.

And the happy terrible mysteries, of the wilds and the wild beasts, the chronicles, and the lion exhibited at the fair, as a conquered enemy, crude but more human than preserving them in the zoological garden; man was alone now on earth, subjugated and destroyed was all else, and the modern terror was the terror in himself.

A stagecoach leaving London, it would be seven in the morning, he would come out of the inn, baskets with fried chicken and wine, and east they would go, the sun rising over the trees and the layers of mist evaporating from the fields. Late in the evening they would wake up from the rattle of the wheels over the cobbles of Dover, and in the morning he would sail across; and then in, deep into the heart of Europe, the feeling of land, trees, and towns all around you, an enclosing, a security of being taken in. East and south to the heart of France, Dijon, the shock of that idea of men living their lifetime in a little town upon which you suddenly came, so far from the seas, so remote, men looking at the earth from that place as from its centre. The velvet night, wandering along the walls, the clear sounds of bells and voices, the meeting of a lady with her maid on their evening walk –

*

While he shaved he thought: Thank heaven, it's Monday again; and his thoughts went on: But I'm not on the right path, it is ridiculous to torment myself these week-end days, and then to show it to Catherine on Monday is all wrong, all wrong. God, why are we always set on what we have not got?

I have an affair, I like the sound of that word, I have a lot to do in this wild and messy world, I must stop vegetating, burn brightly, the light of ideas. A beautiful woman lets me make love to her, she gives me her body and what more could a man want, no entangled emotions, a clear making of each other complete.

It was past nine o'clock. He had had his hand on the receiver when these thoughts stopped him from telephoning Catherine, and he hastened out of the house to remove himself from that hesitation. He went to class at ten, out at eleven; there was another one in his department from twelve until one and he had never gone to both because he always found it too inconvenient either to come twice or to wait for an hour at the university. He now decided to attend the other class too. He looked at the bulletin board to select a lecture to fill the time in between and chose an hour on Medieval French, but it turned out to be very un-Villonesque and a discussion of S before T to which he stopped listening after a few minutes. He was going to telephone Catherine after one, but he now thought, twelve is late enough too, the thing which mattered was not to call her first thing in the morning. So he walked down the marble corridor at the noon intermission, and got her on the telephone. She sounded pleased to hear his voice, but he was determined to keep to his new regime.

'I'm sorry, Cath, I can't make it at five,' he told her, and when her voice sounded surprised and perhaps hurt, he added something about a Hollandia dinner although he had promised himself not to give any reasons. 'May I see you later, at ten or eleven? Yes, all right, half past nine then, I'll come for you.'

Now that it was done he felt a fool. Well, I knew I would, he said to himself, but damn it. I'll only hang around from five to nine, is it worth-while? Can I play this role of someone who I obviously am not? Catherine sounded so surprised and it didn't make me happy that my scheme worked, I only felt apologetic.

It seemed important now not to miss the other class, and he hastily walked to it, his shoes slipping on the stone floor, and asked his neighbour for a piece of paper and filled it with notes, and stars, and decorated C's.

Anthoni paid the bill for his Hollandia meals but none of his other debts, and he omitted paying these not like the reckless Student of Prague, but as a rather desperate means of keeping some money in his pocket, a need he suddenly experienced with urgency. He went to get Catherine who had been waiting for him with her coat already on, telling him that she had been in her room all day and was dying to get out. He apologized again for not being able to come sooner, and his eyes went around the room and to the closed bedroom door, how strange, it was always ajar, thinking of the man who had been there the day before and perhaps the night and the morning. They walked the still street until they were both cold on that chilly and melancholy evening, and went to the Tonhalle to drink coffee, talking quietly at a table in a corner, surrounded by a lake of empty chairs, Catherine speaking about her stay in England, mostly spent in very respectable boarding-houses for young ladies, and he about a pre-war holiday visit to Switzerland.

'I'm weary,' Catherine said, 'I am at an impasse. I didn't know this morning what to do next, and I have made sketches all day. But I think now that I've got something. I can't talk about it yet.'

'Shall we go to my room?'

'Yes, I want that. I can't face mine yet, especially not after the dreadful things I drew there today.'

At Bellevue they took the streetcar up. What a strange homecoming, Anthoni thought, we are sitting here so tired and unexcited, and for all that there is a kind of intimacy in that very state. We are going home, he said to himself, as if we lived in Culmann street, as if we had been married for a long time, as if there was a home of both of us.

*

The grey light that immediately precedes sunrise on a cloudy day filled the room. He regarded Catherine's head on the pillow, so close to him in the small bed, her hair still straightly and neatly going out and leaving her face all free, her left arm on the cover, her hand touching the wall. He kept very silent, but she opened her eyes and looked at him, wide awake, then closed them and made a kissing movement. He brought his head nearer until he touched her mouth with his lips, and lay like that for a while, a great tenderness moving him. Catherine did not remain still, and she put her hands out towards him. He waited with closed eyes, a closed face, then he let himself glide down and he kissed her, hesitatingly. She let her hand move through his hair, and said, come, but he could not. After that he stayed motionless, and then came up to her face, holding her tight now, both arms around her, and he said, almost crying: 'Oh my dear girl, oh my dear girl, forgive me, please,' and she smiled at him with a smile full of effort.

He was startled by a knock on the door. Nobody ever came to his room and it was very early. Damn her, the landlady, he thought, and called out in a hoarse, angry voice: 'What is it?'

'Telephone, sir,' a flat woman's voice answered.

'I'm coming,' Anthoni muttered, 'please tell them to wait.'

It was Day. He could not hide the annoyance in his voice as he replied.

'Hello, Jean-Pierre, you are early – or should I say late?'

Day spoke quickly and in a harsh voice.

'Toni,' he said, 'the invasion has just begun.'

'No,' Anthoni said, without thinking yet.

'Four thousand ships are out,' Day almost shouted, for once having all the details in his grasp. 'They are bombarding the coast and landing troops by ship and from planes. This is it, my friend.'

'Where?' Anthoni asked.

'Normandy. It's no raid, I heard the proclamation. It's the beginning of the end, Toni. A friend of mine called me, I was asleep too,' he added with his little laugh. 'You are the first one I'm phoning.'

Anthoni was silent for what seemed to himself a long time. This then was the day, this strange morning the morning so waited for.

How often had he thought about what he would do, how many plans made with others, images rising before his mind, half-dreamed, crossing the border, breaking through the lines, liberation, such a glory. But it was all there still, a continent, his own little storms of no account, a desperately abided day which could bring no disappointments; and then what? How mental his reaction was, how he seemed not to partake any more in the vast movement of light against darkness, he had been so ready for it, to die for it. He felt weird, he did not know what else to say to Jean-Pierre, it was too late now to shout for joy, and he only murmured, the invasion, well, my God ... and then he asked: 'Where will you be, can I see you?' and Day said he should come, of course, he could go with him to Geneva probably, if he wanted that.

'I'll pass by later then,' Anthoni ended and hung up.

He went back to his room and locked the door without Catherine looking up at him, and sat on the bed and bent his eyes on hers which were big and cool grey and like those of someone who was hurt and had retreated into herself.

'Jean-Pierre,' he said. 'The invasion started this morning.'

'The invasion,' Catherine repeated, in a half-questioning voice, and pursed her lips.

He got up and walked to the window and he looked out over the empty street. The day was overcast, it had rained before dawn.

*

There was an extra edition at Bellevue and apart from that the town was quiet. Perhaps as quiet as usual but to Anthoni it seemed deadened with silence because he had expected throngs in the street, visible emotion. Even his streetcar passengers were silently staring ahead as always. He only heard two men exchanging some words on the subject: 'Well, one must wait and see, it's easier to make a landing than to stay,' and when he got off he made his way through them as roughly as possible, with a frown on his face, muttering an oath about damned Swiss complacency. And then his own mood re-emerged, and Day was surprised to see his face. 'Toni,' he cried, 'don't be afraid, you'll be in time to give a hand' – not thinking of any other reason for Anthoni's gloomy expression – 'it's enormous, my friend, there is not a railway bridge left over the Seine . . . It will all be over soon now,' he continued, without bothering about the contradiction between this statement and his first words. He was pacing through his room, fixing his tie and glancing in the mirror every time he passed it. A suitcase was open on the couch. 'I'm going to Geneva at five, great things will happen.'

'Could I really come with you?' Anthoni asked almost involuntarily, for though he had told himself that he would make up his mind about it after having seen Day, he knew somewhere that he did not want to leave Zurich now.

'Yes of course, I counted on that. It would be very strange if we couldn't manage you somehow. I'm almost certain I'll go to France too. You can have lunch with me if you want to and accompany me on my errands. I have a lot of things to do.'

'So would I if I'm leaving at five,' Anthoni replied automatically.

'Let's think then where we can meet,' Jean-Pierre said.

'Well,' Anthoni began, 'now, first of all, how sure is it that I can get through?'

Jean-Pierre was taken aback by this prudent and dull question on such a day. 'Sure,' he said, 'nothing is sure, Toni, but if you just –' and he made a gesture with a clenched fist to indicate the spirit in which the thing should be undertaken.

'Yes, but you see,' Anthoni went on, 'I have very little money, as you are bound to know by now, and *ad nauseam* too. I really couldn't manage to stay in Geneva for more than a few days, and then there is my room here with my things . . .'

'I don't know about that,' Day answered with a bit less enthusiasm, 'I could lend you something, of course . . .'

'Oh no,' Anthoni hastened to interject, 'no, I don't want that.'

'You might be able to stay with Lennard for some time – I'm not sure, I think he might have a girl friend staying with him.'

Anthoni sat down, I have to think fast, he told himself, it is one of those now or never moments, there just can't be any conflict here, I must forget about everything else. I'm really like a prisoner of war with the duty to escape as soon as possible.

I have to pay some debts before leaving, give up my room, put my things somewhere, the consul won't like this at all, I could never manage it before five. Yes I could, of course I could, I don't need anything, my landlady can inherit the lot, what does it matter? But then – to Geneva, I'll begin by buying a third-class ticket, it will be like a demonstration and Jean-

Pierre will offer to supplement the difference, we'll arrive late, he'll dine on the train and I'll refuse his invitation: and then the hotel, too late for other arrangements ... He saw the arrival in Geneva, Day getting off the train and striding along the platform in his fitted grey suit, black hat, a porter following with his luggage, the doorman at the hotel evaluating him properly and making a bow to money, and he standing there, shifting his tie over the stain on his shirt, waiting for Jean-Pierre to telephone Lennard about a room, Jean-Pierre accosted by old friends, distracted, looking at the women in the lobby, telling him not to be a fusspot for one night and take a room in the hotel, too. And he reflected that the room-clerks and the landladies would be this day so frightfully much the same as any other day.

Then he realized with a shock that in all these musings he had forgotten again about the invasion, had thought of it all as of a trip – to Geneva, the Zuricher station at five the big clock, the hand on five, we are moving, the last view of the houses of Zurich. And then he knew that he could not separate himself now from Catherine. He did not understand why, but he knew instinctively and unmistakably that he would never see her again if he left that day.

'I have to go out,' Day said, 'you want to come down with me?'

Anthoni followed him and walked beside him down Seefeld street. 'You know what, Jean-Pierre,' he finally said, 'I'll wait here first, and I'll phone you tomorrow night to find out how things are. Does that suit you?'

'But I don't know where I'll be,' Day answered rather gruffly.

Anthoni was silent, he cursed himself, and hunched his shoulders and thought, let them all go to hell, I have done more and waited longer for this invasion than most of them, I'll be there; and he replied: 'Can't you give me Lennard's phone number? I'll call you there and perhaps you can leave a message for me. I just have no money for anything which is not absolutely sure. And,' he ended, 'I don't want to leave

Catherine if I don't have to. I mean just to hang around in Geneva.'

Jean-Pierre nodded in answer, and smiled at him more warmly.

*

He left Jean-Pierre at the Quay Bridge and crossed the river, going slowly, looking over the grey lake on which the wind blew streaks of ripples. He could not go to the university today, that was certain, nor did he want to see Ellis who would expect him to be in too different a frame of mind from his present one.

Zurich was now acquiring a new aspect again, and he was astonished to find that even the idea of leaving the town itself was not attractive any more. He had not used his opportunities, he should have worked hard, got past the staring at formulas, really know, but then, wasn't it all the same and only a matter of a diploma; his physics, this 'mathematical description of the world' – how tedious it had turned out to be – he should have stopped long ago, no, finished it quickly first and then submerged himself in human things, the history, the mysteries of Europe. His eyes were opened to that only now, there was the limitation of the small Swiss town but he had forgotten the million books all around him; he saw an image, an abstraction of writing, a time of inspiration, Catherine's painting, a high unison.

He had arrived at the little park where the Mythen Quay begins and sat down in the wet grass, and then forced his mind along more rational lines. 'Time to grow up,' he said aloud. 'This is my catechism: Zurich is a backwater; the middle of the great war is not the time for scholarship; I'll see Catherine again if I really want to and try '

Later he walked along the embankment to a newspaper office. He reread the bulletins in the window several times, weighing the words, the German communiqué in its assurance hung next to the Allied one. He then started on the advertisements, leaning on the window sill. If he left he would have to give up his room, and finding somebody to take it over would mean almost a month's rent saved, and that money might be terribly important. There were however many rooms offered and only a few demanded.

A handful of people were hanging around the office, a sad crowd mostly, see, it's true, only bums have time here, he thought. One of these suddenly tugged violently at his sleeve and began to talk to him in a heavy mountain dialect of which he could not understand a word. Anthoni shook his head, saying no, no, I'm sorry, and began walking up the street in big steps. He entered a telephone booth, I am going to call up Jean-Pierre, he thought, I'm going with him all the same, and start anew, I'll just pick up a shirt at home and my toilet things. But he could not quite make it, he was standing in the booth, his back against the door, flipping the twenty-centime piece, groaning almost, God, what to do, what to do. He ended by calling Catherine.

'I'm in a complete turmoil,' he said to her, and then suddenly making up his mind: 'I was supposed to leave today, to Geneva first, but I'm not going. Now I'll phone them tomorrow night, and then I'll know more.'

'Are you sure that is the best thing, Toni?' Catherine asked, as if she were discussing an abstract problem.

'Yes, I'm sure,' Anthoni whispered.

'Will you come to me afterwards then,' she replied, her voice now sounding warm, 'or you can phone from here if you want to.'

'You are sweet,' Anthoni said inaudibly, and cleared his throat, and said again: 'You are sweet.'

*

All the following day he was on the street, eating a lunch of rolls on a bench at the lake, spelling the papers, even wandering through the Museum of National Art and Culture. These were hard hours. At six he went to the nonalcoholic restaurant and ate something called Birchermuesli which was the cheapest item on the menu and tasted that way. Then finally the moment came to go and telephone Day.

He was connected quickly and the voice at the other end of the line caught him unawares. 'Is Mr Day there perhaps?' he asked in English, then, correcting himself, in French, and it took him some time to realize that it was Day himself who had answered the telephone.

'Hello, Toni,' he said, 'how are you my friend? How is your lovely girl?'

'Jean-Pierre,' Anthoni answered, pleased by Day's personal presence, but slightly taken aback by the jolly conversational beginning of what he had expected for thirty-six hours to be a momentous call, 'tell me, how is the situation?'

'The situation,' Jean-Pierre repeated in his gay pre-invasion voice, 'the situation is well in hand. I'm sitting here with the most beautiful woman you have ever seen' – there was talking and laughing – 'but,' he continued, 'it is like this, Toni. You were right when you decided to wait. The Swiss have closed their border so hermetically that even our men can't get through. Those here who know do not even expect the Allied bridgehead to be considerably enlarged before the end of the month. Our wait isn't over yet.'

'Oh damn it all,' Anthoni said.

'I was in a pretty desperate way myself last night,' Day answered, 'there I was, finally all set for the great denouement, and then, pss, this cold shower. But I now see it in a better perspective, war is no joke, Toni, and we will have plenty of it. The Jerries aren't beaten by far ..'

The operator announced the end of three minutes.

'Jean-Pierre,' Toni shouted hastily, 'wait, are you sure? Wouldn't it make a difference if I came to Geneva after all?'

'Not a bit. I'm coming back myself tomorrow.'

He walked to Tal street, muttering, how disgusting, how stupid, but though he did not admit it to himself, he was very relieved. There was no point in crossing yet, and he could put his life in order without a sense of guilt, of wasted chance. A month seemed a very long time, in a month from now he could leave wholeheartedly. The war would probably last through the winter then – what a terrible creature is man, he suddenly thought, man is a wolf to man, each week the war lasts longer is a week of death, and here I am, counting off the bloody months against my own interests – and yet, and yet, are many people having such thoughts, are the many really so cruel? I wouldn't lengthen the war a day, even if a day longer in Zurich would mean everything to me, but I would be secretly hoping for that day, secretly to myself. So he came to her house.

'Catherine,' he said, 'why do you look so gloomy? I've never seen you like this.'

'I've prepared myself mentally for a good-bye,' she answered with a smile.

'But I'm not going, I called Geneva just now, it turns out that nothing has changed, it might take a long time still, half a year ... I'm sorry about yesterday morning, Catherine, we had a bad night, it left me very sad, and you too. We'll do better, you are not sick of me, are you?'

She put out her hand and made him sit next to her on the couch, she stroked his hair away from his forehead and lifted her face to be kissed.

Going home from her that night he decided to move to another room, and the next morning he told his landlady. Whatever would happen, the indefiniteness of the war was ended and the waiting had changed character. What he had found himself unable to do right away put, now postponed, the coming days in a new relief in which many things did not matter much any more, and one of these was money. He wanted a better place, for Catherine, he needed a room in which his own spirit would be discernible, and no oppressive landlady's eye on his doings; he would be able to receive her in a room like that. It would make very much of a change not to be confined any longer to his role as a guest in Tal street, where the idea of the man from Zug might become some sort of obsession. On the back page of his notebook he added his expenses. Even if he would use as much as a hundred francs of his money for rent he could manage on the rest, he could sell more things, let his debts wait. A hundred francs was enough for a very good room.

*

Life seemed paradoxically more normal now that he was waiting for the day to cross the border to France with Jean-Pierre than it had when there was nothing left to wait for except his own decision to go, unaided, nothing to give him a sense of waiting but the feeling of guilt at not partaking in the great war.

That afternoon he set out with the newspaper advertisements, having decided to look only at those rooms which were in the centre of town. He had never lived there, he had always stayed in the university section like all the students; to move downtown was in its small way an essential change. Zurich, the day, his life would be different, seen from a different vantage point.

The second address he visited was in Tal street itself, just around the corner from Parade Square. It was several blocks from Catherine's apartment, but that was all for the best, he would never want to move too close to her, that would be like laying a siege. It was a good room, looking over the square, with its own entrance outside the door of the pension, in a modern building with an elevator, unusual for Zurich, and there was something incongruous in its businesslike aspect, in the idea of sleeping and brushing one's teeth twenty feet from the main square of Zurich. It cost a hundred and ten francs. This is madness, he thought, I can't spend half my income on rent. 'I'll come back later,' he said.

He walked to the square and waited for a streetcar to his next address, but when it arrived he did not get on it. I'll save by not running out every minute, he told himself, I'll eat in my room, a cheap room is really the more expensive one. I'll certainly go less to Hollandia now that I'm out of that neighbourhood. It's for such a short time. A year from now I may be dead.

He hurried back, someone else might just then be taking the place, and rented it. They agreed on a hundred francs for the rest of the month, which left him with six francs.

It was evening when he returned to Culmann street but he was determined to complete his break that day. On the way up the street he had borrowed another suitcase at Hollandia, and he now had three, which should be enough for his possessions. He put his things on the bed, scrutinizing them in the process.

When he had first come to Zurich he had only some toilet articles and a raincoat, and there had been a kind of exhilaration in that. I never want to possess more than what fits into one suitcase, he had believed; he had thought of his full closets left behind in Amsterdam and reflected that he didn't miss any of all those so necessary belongings, that the world was far and wide and property an anchor in the mud.

He could now remember those feelings but could not feel them, for he seemed in need of so much. He regretted that Catherine could not see him better dressed, and missed all the thing which would have made his new Parade Square room more personal.

His landlady knocked and came in. Some springs in the mattress were broken, she told him with a fleeting scowl, and she expected payment for that. He said: Wasn't that in the normal wear and tear of a furnished room? Well, the bed wasn't, the mattress wasn't, meant for two persons, she finally answered.

I wondered when she would get down to that, Anthoni thought, here it is, blackmail! and he smiled for that word seemed to accentuate the ridiculousness of it all. 'I don't see any broken springs,' he replied, 'and I haven't a penny anyway. Besides, I've paid for the whole month.'

After that he packed in a hurry, expecting her to reappear and make trouble somehow; he had one and a half suitcases full of books, one with his clothes, a sad lot they were, odds

105

and ends, a pistol an interned English officer had given him, a pair of skis. The books' suitcase was desperately heavy. He opened the door to the corridor, which was empty, and the entrance door, and he carried everything out into the staircase.

He let his eyes go around his room once more, he touched the pillow. Then he quickly closed both doors behind him. Nobody had interfered with his departure.

*

A man was writing a letter in the locked backroom of a French bakery in a hamlet north and west of Valence. It was just getting light, he had come during the night on foot and his shoes were covered with white dust from the long dry path that wound down from the hills to this house which was the first one on the road coming in. The letter was for Geneva.

'I know as well as you, Pierre,' he wrote, 'that there is no mastermind behind the Maquis, but right now it looks like it. The cumulative effect of our actions could certainly be no greater. In the three days since the invasion I have spoken to more of our men than in the whole of the winter. Near Dijon both tracks to Paris were destroyed over a length of one hundred yards. It happened that a train with repair materials had to be sent all the way from Marseille, and by coincidence it was this train which was attacked and derailed here, between Valence and Lyon. All this is blocking their transport system in a geometrical progression ...

'... this comes to you via Vallorbe. We try to find a new way to Geneva, we need pharmaceuticals and ammunition.'

The sun was well over the horizon and its warmth could already be felt, the hedges threw long shadows over the roads, and far through the trees a glitter could be perceived which was the river Rhône. There was a haze of dust on the path through the village, a German soldier with a rifle across his back was bicycling along the silent houses which had their paintless shutters closed; next to him came a man in a rain-

coat, half walking, half running to keep up with him. Where
the houses ended the man crossed the road and stood still
behind a tree. He pointed to the bakery. 'There he is,' he said
to the soldier.

*

Anthoni walked with Catherine along Tal street, back to his
room, in the changing light of an evening of which the sky was
now filled with clouds, then again with vast figures of green-
blue.

'What has happened to you, Toni?' Catherine had asked.
'You look so new.'

'That's the most perfect thing you could say to me, Cath.
I'm turning over new leaves every other day, and it never
shows; finally I have hit one that does,' he said in a happy
voice. 'I guess it's nothing more, though, than that I'm well-
shaven for once. I have the pleasure to inform you that I've
now moved into a hot-water neighbourhood.'

There was an excitement in going to his room with her
which was more than the clearness of entering a big hall, unlocking his own door without looking left or right, not listening
to voices, not apprehensive of intervention. He was not yet
used to his actually living there, he still caught himself in the
vague notion that he had to go back up to the students' streets
at the other side of the river, and it was a pleasure then to
realize that it was not so. He could find no fault with the
place.

He stood next to her in the entrance and said: 'It's a good
room isn't it, Catherine? Not beautiful, but it's real furniture
it has some line, and that's a great miracle. You don't know
the horrors they call furnished rooms.'

They sat on the window sill together and looked down on
Parade Square over which dusk was now closing. The air was
almost still, there was a sound of faraway voices and the light
ting of a streetcar bell. Then the lights of the square flashed on
and the bluish greyness suddenly became yellow, the streetcars became bundles of light rounding the corners, and the

advertisements, red, yellow, and white neon, threw a succession of colours on their faces and on the walls and ceiling of the room.

They turned towards each other and smiled at the same moment. 'It's a happy room,' Catherine said softly, and he thought: How strange, I am convinced of the power of the mind and all that, the moving force of an emotion, and here I find a place being more important than anything else, all is new, truly so. Shouldn't I have been able to renew our being together in Culmann street, in a dingy old attic even? But then he felt just grateful for his luck, for having arranged all this, and said to himself, I'll leave well enough alone. He held out his hand which she took, and in the coloured lights she looked different from any way he had ever seen her, a warm unasking gentleness, and it was not a mood of hers but of them both, made together.

After a long time Catherine said: 'I'm going to my parents in Schaffhausen for the week-end'; and he wondered whether she had decided that before or just then, but knew that it meant there should be no shadow of tomorrow for you on this night, because I will not see him tomorrow. He said dreamily, not reflecting farther than these thoughts: 'I'd like to come with you.'

'You can if you really want to,' Catherine answered, 'but you won't like it. It's a big house and during the week-ends it's filled with people, and not the kind you'd enjoy Elderly men with too much money and wives with too much leisure time to be frustrated in.'

'Oh, I know how that is,' Anthoni replied. 'My parents' house used to be like that during the summer months. We lived quite close to Amsterdam. All sorts of horrible people used to consider us a convenient week-end resort.'

He was exaggerating, but her words had made him think that he should boast a bit about himself. He had never talked about his parents or his background with her and he did so now because he felt sure that he was able to speak in a light-handed way which made it sound natural.

Catherine hesitated and then she said: 'All right then, it's settled. You are coming with me, and you'll face the music. You mustn't mind, though, when I introduce you as an acquaintance.'

'An acquaintance, Cath?' Anthoni asked, and he let his hand glide over her hair and down her back. 'No, I don't really want to go,' he added, 'I'm not social enough for such occasions. But tell me about them.'

'My father is a dark and small man,' she said, 'he has a definitely distinguished air. I like him. My sister lives in Bern, she is a divorcee and she has a fulltime job spending all her money.'

'Does she look like you?'

'She is taller, and she is getting rather heavy I'm afraid. She is considered the greater beauty of us two. My mother' – she paused – 'has made my father and us rather miserable. Things are more peaceful now. He has wrapped himself up in isolation, and I see her only when I go to Schaffhausen. I'm doing my best, and we behave in a civilized way. She has given me a bad childhood. She used to beat me, with her hairbrush. I lived in terror of her. She is completely hysterical of course.'

Catherine laughed her short soft laugh. 'Doesn't it sound a bit like Ibsen? You must be getting afraid of me. I can tell you, I'm from a dreadful family. She used to say to me that I was ugly and that my only chance was to study, and that there was a devil in me. Once when I looked at myself in the mirror of her bedroom she hit me with a hot curling-iron.' Catherine spoke in her amused anecdotal voice. 'Now you can imagine,' she continued, 'what sort of monster I was when I came out of school. I had been thoroughly beaten into a timid and wicked girl. I had a paralyzing sense of inferiority. Then my father finally woke up to the fact that he should do something about me, and sent me to England. It didn't change me much for I was practically ignored there, I was hopelessly unpopular. But it freed me from my mother. When I came back I refused to stay with them, and in the end she had to give in and let me live in Zurich. Then I had my operation, although she forbade it and even phoned the doctors to stop them.' Catherine touched her breasts for a moment with one hand. 'It was quite a thing, it lasted three hours. Now I have my scars of course.'

'You have very beautiful breasts, Catherine,' Anthoni said softly.

Catherine closed her eyes for a second. 'You know the rest, I found out that I could draw . . . I don't think I'll ever forgive her for my youth, though.'

'What a terrible pity, Cath.'

'Yes, it's supposed to be the best time of your life.' Catherine remarked. 'I think there are compensations though. I have no attachments and I like that. I never want to be dependent again. They have given me that at least with their money. I am free. But I am not very strong,' she added. 'I still need the strength of others. You look very strong this night, Toni.'

He smiled at her, and then there was a long silence. 'Shall we go to bed?' he asked.

'I like these lights,' she said, 'I'll leave the curtains open. I want to see you. You are a beautiful man.'

'Is there such a thing?' he whispered.

'Yes, there is.'

He kissed her body, until she had come to the top, and then he could still wait for her again.

'Lie on my shoulder,' he asked her, 'I want to hold you.'

He held her very tight in his arms, staring up at the ceiling in its changing from white to yellow to red, he thought of days gone by, he saw himself in his bed as a child, trying with his feet to reach the end and worrying that he would not grow any more. A third of my life is gone, he thought. He kissed Catherine, who was almost asleep, in her hair, and suddenly his eyes filled with tears and he was sinking in a surge of tenderness, and love, for her.

The past; never knowing quite what to believe of the adventures of his friends, he had always realized that he was far behind them, his thoughts about love and about woman had not a single tie with his reality Those things had never been mentioned by his parents, a discussion of them completely out of the question, but he had read every book that came in the house and nobody had interfered with that. Once alone in his mother's bedroom he had discovered a French novel in her closet which was called *Love for Three,* and was illustrated with photographs. He had tried to read it with his grade-school French, his heart pounding, putting it back in place whenever he heard a sound, and for a time afterwards he had made secret trips to the closet, never finishing the book but looking up the passages of the photographs and rereading them. Much later, in high school, somebody had lent him *Lady Chatterley's Lover,* the real one, the boy had said, and he had read it that night, feverishly skipping through the pages while searching for 'it', until suddenly he was disgusted with himself and with the book too; and the next morning he had given it back to the boy before school in a need to get rid of it. Nobody had believed that motive, of course, they had assumed he was afraid his mother might discover it, and he had vainly defended himself. At the time, or perhaps it was a year or more afterwards, a girl had come to sew in the neighbour's house he could still visualize her quite well, very round and firm, almost plump, and there was something vulgar in her which put her in a class with women in books, entirely separated from schoolgirls; he had had wild and vague dreams in which they were both lying naked on a bed. Once when he was coming home she stood in the doorway, and he had dropped a book just there, and a passing child had kicked it away. He had shouted; 'Damn you,' and she had said: 'That is not a nice word to use,' but looked at him in surprise when he answered: 'I'm sorry.' Those were the only words he had ever spoken to her. He had not kissed a girl until he was eighteen or nineteen, and all those years he had had a sense of comfort in his unseenness. Thinking himself ugly, or clumsy, he had known that it should be all preparation, years of apprenticeship, for the great meeting. He would have to learn many things, driving a car, dancing, his socks would have to be without holes and his body tanned. His standards for himself had ranged from the most childish ones upwards, he thought, and it had been long before he had stopped thinking of dashing feats as the way to a woman and, for the first time, had felt someone's eyes on him because of something he had said, not something he had done. It had been such a glorious conception, the silent preparation, completing oneself, storing ideas, building, so much to give, all waiting, expecting. The meeting, the meeting of her.

*

Ingeborg regarded him with an inquisitive look and said, 'There is something changed about him, and I don't know what yet'; and she did not listen when Robert Ellis made some mild joke that Anthoni just looked hungry and that hunger was now the only thing which drove him to them. 'We had expected you on the big day,' Robert continued, 'and don't tell me you only show up on Sunday because you have been working all week. This time we'll not pretend to believe that.'

'Sunday is my visiting day,' Anthoni said solemnly, and added without explaining further, 'I'm sorry I couldn't look in sooner.'

'We decided that you were having tea in London by now.'

'There was a lot of commotion,' Anthoni replied, 'but it has all died down again. I have to stay a while longer, and I don't quite mind, we are actually waiting for the clearing of a passage out. The Swiss put their frontier zone in a state of alarm. I decided I shouldn't jeopardize everything for the sake of some weeks, and spend the rest of the war in a Swiss jail.'

'You have plenty of time, Toni,' Ingeborg said with a sigh, 'it isn't over by far.'

They talked about the invasion and the chances for a German internal breakdown, and he thought, these are vital

112

matters, I am saying more or less sensible things about them, yet this is not me, sitting here, not my real-now-self. Are Ingeborg and Robert truly preoccupied with this, or do they talk about it because I am supposed to be the politics and seriousness man? Why on earth do they seem to like me? As a matter of fact, I have always been a terrible bore with them. They are so cool to each other today. What is their real relation? Ingeborg likes me in an intimate way, but completely asexual, there is a contradiction in it. 'How are you these days Ingeborg?' he suddenly asked.

She looked surprised at him. 'I only have to go back for a check-up in a year from now,' she then said. 'But I hope I won't be here to see that day.'

Ellis said: 'Ingeborg has now taken it into her head to go to Hollywood. I don't quite see how she thinks she will manage, working under pressure, although she ...'

'Please, Robbie, no symptomcy,' Ingeborg interrupted him.

'Hollywood,' Anthoni said, 'I certainly think you should be able to get through to America in a year from now. What is wrong with the idea?'

'There is nothing wrong with it,' Robert answered icily, looking at her, 'only she'll have to go alone.'

'I'm willing to go,' Anthoni said cheerfully, and Ingeborg looked at him with a musing smile which made him uncomfortable, the wrong thing to say, he thought and avoided noticing Robert's reaction. 'Why don't you want to go to Hollywood, Robert? Don't you want a swimming-pool?'

'I am not going to live in the United States,' Ellis said slowly, obviously repeating lines from an argument with Ingeborg.

'And I am,' she said.

'I'm not judging its merits, it just so happens that it's not the place for me. I am not modern enough,' Ellis continued, looking from her to Anthoni.

'Don't look at me,' Anthoni said, 'I'm not one of the modernists.'

Ellis was silent and then he said: 'I have a good example to illustrate my point. You should appreciate this, Ingeborg, it's film. The humour of a country is a very specific thing,' he went on, looking at Anthoni. 'Now take film humour. In American films mirth is provided by human beings who run up against the world of things. Fred MacMurray struggling with a waffle iron. The people are funny because they don't know how to handle these things which, in themselves, are never questioned. Is that granted?'

They did not answer, and he went on: 'In European films the same situations are used to provide humour, but the accent has been shifted. Here the things, the machines, the institutions, become ridiculous in their inhumanness. I may be a reactionary,' he ended, 'but I prefer the culture of the latter point of view, to live in that is.'

Anthoni and Ingeborg looked at each other and then for no reason suddenly burst out laughing. Anthoni blushed scarlet. 'I'm dreadfully sorry, Robert, he managed to say, 'I'm not laughing at you at all, I like your film-argument, I really don't know what is the matter with us . . .'

He glanced at Ellis, who smiled, a sincere, natural smile. You are a nice man, Anthoni thought. He sensed his own feeling of lightness and happiness then so very acutely, he had the right not to bother, his time of troubles would come, right now he just could not be miserable about anything. The world was a mess, but man, suffering man himself, had made it that. To each his turn for the endeavour. 'Endeavour,' he suddenly shouted. 'That was the name my canoe had. That's long ago. It was called after some famous yacht. That name used to stun the local population.'

'You are completely mad today, Toni,' Ingeborg exclaimed. 'You'd better tell us your secret.'

'Ah, mystery,' he said, saying to himself: I'm loved, I'm in love, I'm in love.

*

It was a brilliant day with a sharp clear sky, the warmth was of radiance and in the prismatic passage of shadow along the houses it was cold. How good it feels to taste time, Anthoni told himself going home, know of the minutes, not to wait for what must come, but be, see yourself move over the earth, a minuscule mass over a minuscule distance, yet present in the universe, here in actuality.

He was carrying a stack of books to his room, this morning he had made his expedition to the central library at the other side of the Limmat which he had been postponing for so long, and within half an hour he had compiled an overwhelming list of books he had always wanted to read; just having made that list had been a completion, a blow to the vague notion that he would go through his life thinking I should do this, I never got down to that, until on his deathbed his heart would break in the thought that it was too late, too late in all eternity.

He had to stop at twelve books because of regulations; he was taking home two volumes on the French revolution, the *Decameron* in German, the *Wealth of Nations*.

He dropped the books on his bed and before closing the door took up a note from the table. Miss Valois had telephoned, it said. He washed, hurriedly because of the open door; he reflected that he looked pale and rubbed his face. Then he left in haste, and locked the door again, the elevator was still on his floor, he got in and smiled at himself in the mirror.

'Hello, my Catherine,' he said breathlessly, 'I was going to phone you but then I realized that I had to see you, so I ran over. Forgive me, I'll fly out again, two minutes.' He talked quickly, while coming into the room, she was standing with her back against the window, a pencil in her left hand, her head held sideways and looking at him. 'I want to draw you,' she said, 'will you pose for me tonight?'

When he came at nine Catherine had rearranged the lights and the couch was moved, a black shawl was a dark background. 'When I'm working I'm very businesslike,' she said, with the accent on 'very', in her high voice with the pitch of amusement at herself.

'I always assumed painters made love to their models,' Anthoni said.

'You have to stand in that corner,' she told him, 'I had an electric fire brought up in case you get cold.'

Anthoni felt oddly shy and excited at the same time. 'You want me undressed?' he asked.

'Yes, I'll give you a dressing-gown.'

He took his clothes off in the bedroom, a strange experience, so very different from undressing with her. He put the dressing-gown on and stepped into the other room, making an effort to walk naturally and overcome an awkwardness which had taken possession of him. 'I'm very cold,' he said, 'I'll put that fire on first.'

He was to stand against the wall, leaning with one elbow on a cabinet. Catherine sat opposite him with her sketchbook, and she put on the glasses which he had seen her wear only once before, for a few minutes in the cabaret. They gave her an intellectual face without disturbing its lines. 'You are standing very gracefully,' she said. 'You must tell me if you have to move.'

He regarded her, drawing, and then his own body, there was a desire rousing in him and then ebbing away again, in a rhythm almost, and embarrassment made him try to concentrate on something quite different. But his mind kept returning to himself, the idea of her seeing his excitement. Passion, he reflected, if you asked how it works, one would say that a man gets excited by looking at a woman, but there is a more dissolute feeling which is excitement created by the idea of your own body being seen by a woman.

He suddenly had the sensation of having come upon a basic truth. There are three passions: the reflection on one's self, which is primitive and isolating; then there is that being-seen feeling, and I suppose that is what you would call physical love; and the third is the forgetting one's self, being enrap-

116

tured wholly by the other, and that is a human, real love. And then his thoughts went on, but no, the passions of an animal must be closer to the last than to the second one. The being-seen type is the most human perhaps, who was it, Da Vinci?, who said that there would be no children born if mirrors were hung next to all beds, he certainly couldn't have been more wrong. Only the category of ugly aesthetes would stop making love. That must be a rather small group. He grinned.

Say then that there is no moral difference, that one passion is not more spiritual than another; it tells, though, it tells of one's character and soul, whether you look at the other or at yourself. He now realized for the first time: I have had moments of weakness, and I tilted myself over by this concentration of thought, here I am naked in bed with a naked woman, this is me that is being touched; and so it was not the thought of Catherine, of her beauty and womanness but the thought of myself which moved me. One can be alone then in making love, very much so, it is not in itself a uniting force, it would be a catastrophe if all over the earth men and women started to speak their true, intimate thoughts while being to-gether – women thinking of that day's movie, and men managing to wait longer by forcing their minds on tomorrow's work at the office or possibly visualizing another woman – but what a gigantic tableau this is of a false human relationship. Or is it all a game, does everybody know at heart, am I so naïve? His eyes went to Catherine, and she was observing him with such detachment, so pleasently professional, that he suddenly said, 'Catherine, I am worried, I think you are sort of drawing me out of your system, and when your sketch is finished you won't want to make love to me anymore?' Catherine shook her head with a smile, obviously not quite listening, and she made a gesture of silence by holding her finger against her lips.

When she told him that he could stop posing he sat down next to her on the couch, and felt a pain almost, of desire, in a passive way, he hoped that she would kiss him; but she did not look at him and worked on; then it lessened, and he felt very

117

weak and shivered. 'Go to bed,' Catherine said, 'I'll be with you in a few minutes.'

Later Anthoni lay awake and wondered, how their making love could be labelled complete and yet it had been all but joyless, perhaps it was true then that having studied him for two hours as a painter she could not very well be intrigued with him afterwards; she had wanted him so impersonally, it seemed, and he had experienced an irritation, hard to conquer, because he had not desired to give but only longed to be caressed. Then he began to think about the books that were still lying on his bed as he had left them, and he was caught in a yearning for a clear asceticism, a life of working hard, he saw an empty white-walled room, a desk covered with papers and books, mind is eternal, I think too much of my wearisome body. 'Woman, woman,' he said in a whisper, peering through the dark at the contour of Catherine's head, and then he thought, woman is the centre of creation, and love, sex, is its force, not the only one, I believe, but overtowering; and the countries which know that are the happiest, the South is harmonious, and the North is grim and psychopathic, it chokes on a mixture of taboos and pornography. Closing his eyes he began to build a half-dream, one of the women of a palace had seen and desired him, and he hid in a clothes basket and was carried inside the building, and during the night it was opened soundlessly by her and she led him to a dimly lit room, pressed a dagger in his hand, and he felt the shock as he struck the weapon into the back of the prince.

*

It was light when Anthoni came out in the street. A tiredness which had lain on him like a block of stone was gone, and he felt lightheaded and ready to laugh about anything. There was a drizzle, the pavement was slippery. When he reached his house he stood still in the doorway, considering, and then he decided not to go in but to walk on to Hollandia, they would be up by he time he arrived there. He wondered what kept him so wide awake, and went around the corner, smiling at a woman with newspapers on the square who sleepily held out a paper to him. So he walked, along the silent streets, and he tried to go in a straight line without looking ahead, his face tilted backwards, with almost closed eyes, feeling the sparse drops of rain on his hair and on his skin.

It was a long way, uphill, and when he came to Hollandia the café door was unlocked, he went through without seeing anybody, and slouched in a deep chair in the club room, took off his wet shoes and pushed them out of sight under his chair, and put his feet up, a newspaper around them. He closed his eyes and said aloud, I am happy, I am happy to be alive.

When he went back into the café he saw that it was only five minutes after eight. His appearance caused some surprise. Had he fallen out of bed, the owner's wife asked. 'He hasn't been to bed yet,' Ernst remarked. Anthoni smiled wickedly, and decided to have a big breakfast celebrating the fact that he did not have to pay in cash.

A student entered who was one of the regular breakfasters; he sat down opposite Anthoni, ordered his coffee and opened one of the books he had with him. 'Is Professor Schlieger still ill?' he asked. Anthoni shrugged, he felt slightly contemptuous of this man who had just come out of his virtuous little bed and who was now wondering about Professor Schlieger; he would be shocked, he thought, if he knew that I haven't seen my room since yesterday afternoon.

When the man had finished he collected his books and got up, but seeing that it was too early for his class, he sat down again and looked at Anthoni, searching for something to say. 'Do you know where you're going for your land duty?' he asked him.

Anthoni made a dismissing gesture. 'I wonder whether the Swiss will have the nerve to put us on that again. They should have realized by now that we are on the winning side in this war.'

'That doesn't bother them, their thesis is that the foreign students should be grateful to be here, and that they will be happy to work on the land for three months. I must admit I personally don't mind so much, it's one fifty a day and nothing to spend it on.'

'Yes, if you get a good farmer to work for . . .,' Anthoni murmured. He would be gone before all that.

Later in the morning, while reading a magazine in the club room, he began wondering. Should I phone Day? he thought. No, I'll look in at the consulate. From there I can go home.

Going up the stairs in the building on Falken street he suddenly remembered that he was not shaven. He hesitated, but then he climbed on. He was here now.

'I'd like to see the consul,' he said and sat down on the faded green couch, picking up an old *National Geographic*. He cursed himself, I'm always doing things by halves, I should have prepared this better. Why did I come here looking messy, half asleep, and without the slightest idea of just what to say? That man with his land duty . . . He frowned unhappily when a girl came to ask him in.

The Dutch consul glanced at him with some amazement, and he bent forward in his chair and held a handkerchief against his face as if he had a cold to hide his unshavenness. The consul assured Anthoni that the military attaché was preparing the way for a convoy.

'I know, sir,' Anthoni said, 'I realize that nothing is gained by bothering you. But walking the streets, reading about the battles . . . there is such isolation here . . . sometimes one has the feeling that nothing is being done, that you have to fight for it yourself because no one else cares a damn . .'

'As soon as possible we'll try to get some fifteen students out and across to the Allies, in three or four small groups,' the consul answered rather coolly. 'We need Allied permission; they are not interested in fifteen soldiers, but for us it is important to be represented.'

He was not at liberty to promise anything but it seemed pretty certain to him that Anthoni was in that first convoy. He assumed that Anthoni knew he was under the military attaché's authority and that it was illegal for him to make any

120

private arrangements. Anthoni confirmed this by a sound from behind his handkerchief. He was in a hurry now to get away and was surprised, alarmed almost, at his own attitude.

On his way out he stole the afternoon paper that had just been delivered.

*

After his talk with the consul Anthoni almost automatically avoided Jean-Pierre who, he could assume, was working on their departure, and not knowing the details he could leave it at that, in the pleasant realization that arrangements were being made, for him and without him; and speaking to Day would spoil that, might even show that there had been no developments since Geneva.

Ellis and Ingeborg had invited him for a drink on Saturday at six in the Canova, an expensive bar oddly situated in a residential block behind Bahnhof street; and there they told him that they were going to Ascona where they had rented a house for a month, and that he was invited. 'It is at the lake,' Ingeborg said, 'Lago Maggiore, the house is under the road and you can swim right from our terrace and everything you like. Ascona is cheap, there are no tourists, the place is empty.'

'It sounds lovely,' Anthoni said enviously. They look happy, he thought, but there is something metallic in their gaiety. I am sure Robert arranged this to postpone and, if possible, end the Hollywood debate. I cannot go, shall I tell them why? For a few seconds he was convinced that he would, he heard himself say the very words about Catherine and himself, and he opened his mouth, and began, listen children, but the words came out inaudibly. He took a hasty sip from his glass. 'You are very sweet to ask me,' he said. 'I hope I can come, if only for a week-end. I can't possibly leave Zurich right now.'

Unexpectedly neither of them pursued the subject. I could have gone for a few days, he then told himself, it might have been a very good thing. I am spoiling part of their pleasure in it. I shouldn't become a monomaniac about Catherine. He continued: 'I really will be leaving Switzerland, well, this summer anyway.'

'Is there any news on that?'

'My big hope is Jean-Pierre Day, the man you met once in the Schifflande, remember; if he lets me down there is the Dutch consul who finally seems to be getting active. But I'd hate crossing in a group.'

'You should come to Ascona with us,' Robert suddenly repeated with a smile. 'It won't be long before you can see the English from our place. The woman who owns the house told me that the Italian shore of the lake has already been under the control of the guerillas for several months at a time.'

'How did the Swiss react to that, Robbie?' Ingeborg asked.

'I assume they just ignored the change and saluted their new colleagues at the border with straight faces. I know they didn't let a mouse enter. They don't want to harbour any more Lenins.'

'They have killed a lot of people by refusing them refuge,' Anthoni muttered. 'Holland at least has never done that,' he went on angrily, although nobody had contradicted him, 'they let in every Belgian in the last war, and before this one every German Jew. They fussed, and counted the guilders, but they didn't send them back with innocent faces. It's really unbelievable, this country writes in its papers that it preserves the values which are lost everywhere else . . .'

Robert made a vague gesture. 'If they hadn't closed their borders completely last year,' he remarked, 'they would have a hundred thousand fugitives by now. The ready pretext for Hitler to invade.'

'Hitler doesn't need pretexts, Robbie,' Ingeborg remarked. 'If he does not invade it's because it wouldn't suit his purpose.'

'The Swiss are realists,' Ellis said with some irony, 'and they are proud of it.'

'But we won't forget this,' Anthoni answered loudly, 'their hotels will be empty after the war.'

'Five years from now they will be as full as ever, Toni. When the memoirs are written and read and the documents published everybody will be thoroughly sick of this war and never want to hear about it again.'

'Oh, I don't want to be the starry-eyed idealist,' Anthoni grumbled, 'but I just do not think decency and indecency are such boring topics. And before you say it, that doesn't make me a revolutionary. Although I like the word, especially for me personally. I'm starting new régimes for myself all the time.'

'The trouble with that is,' Ingeborg unexpectedly said, 'that one always pardons the leader of the old régime. He lives to grab power again.'

'We should have a built-in guillotine to liquidate our former selves,' Anthoni answered her.

*

Going home from the bar in the early evening he turned right when he came to Bahnhof street, realizing why, but not letting the thought emerge to the surface. He walked slowly north, the streets were almost quiet, it was dinnertime, but the greater liveliness of Saturday night in that part of the town was in the air. The sky faraway, over the houses at the other side of the street, was red but above his head it was a clear tight coppery green, and he went, looking upwards at every other step. It was a sky of youth, of memories, and he felt a deep and over-whelming nostalgia waiting in him, a nostalgia for he did not know what, and he pushed it away and stepped faster, and then at the corner of Pelikan street he halted. He looked about him, a man and a woman rounded the corner between himself and the houses, he heard her laugh. He stood still for what seemed to him a long time. He had intended to pass through Pelikan street, and then all the way down Tal street. He had intended to go look at Catherine's house, fearing and hoping to see her and to see her man from Zug. But now he found that he could not do it, and he turned around and went back along Bahnhof street. The sky had darkened.

*

He was still half asleep when he was called to the telephone. It was Catherine. 'I hoped you'd still be at home, Toni,' she said. 'I wanted to talk to you before I started working.' 'Hello, Catherine,' Anthoni said hoarsely.

'I have a dreadful cold,' she continued, 'and first I thought I'd stay in bed. But there is so much to do, and I like the light, I didn't want to waste this day. So I decided to let mind triumph over matter, I am going to lock myself in all day and live on hot tea with rum and paint like a fiend and forget about my cold.'

'It even sounds nice, Catherine,' Anthoni replied.

'So you see, if you would have called me later I wouldn't have come to the phone. But I want to see you tonight if I may. I am going to bed early.'

'I'll come to your place then,' Anthoni said 'All the best with you, Cath.'

He was aware of a feeling of envy, he visualized her in her apartment, the maid bringing teas, she was at home to nobody and a whole day ahead of hard work. I don't meet her on equal terms, he thought, she has her life and I am now an accepted part of it, but for me the part has become dominant. I don't dare go to Ascona – I might end up not daring to go to the war.

I lie on my bed before seeing her, I save myself for those hours, I never go to her from somewhere else, she cannot be but first station – I wonder about lovers in novels, they are always so fresh and ready, I'd like to know whether I am different or whether it's just convention to leave out those details; these old gentlemen of fifty years ago who had supper with their girl friends in the private dining-rooms of Maxim's and made love to them after the dessert, didn't they have to go to the washroom after all that eating and drinking? I could never make love with a taste of cheese in my mouth, you have to feel your own body, in a happy clean way –

His thoughts returned to Catherine who would see him after a day of painting. She is a full-time job for me, he thought

124

ironically, I would make a good lover in the old fashion. All I'd need is a thousand a year, as they say in Jane Austen. Catherine, though, is not a woman who can be wooed, I was mistaken when I imagined that I should be very hard: she wouldn't even notice.

She is bound to change later, he then realized suddenly. How strange, it is not difficult to picture Catherine at fifty. Yes, she would be unhappy then in her aloneness, she would fall in love with a memory, with the memory of me perhaps . . .

He was sorry now for Catherine, that was how it came out, sorry for her that she had to grow old. And he said to himself: I would want to protect her against that, shield her against life and death.

She was in bed when he came, wearing a blue bedjacket and a silk scarf, her hair up; there was a blush on her face and she looked very exquisite. She kissed him on his shoulder, 'I don't want you to get my cold,' she said.

He caressed her, and then she sat up and took off her nightgown and her jacket, knotting her scarf around her neck, and it was impossible for him to wait a moment longer and he took her, and in that second was shaken by the sharp and complete change in himself, upset now by his behaviour in what had seemed a deep and inexhaustible passion, so quickly spent, leaving her incomplete. He said: 'Catherine, it has been so many days – please wait.'

He regarded her face, and she smiled happily at him, and he listened to his own body, waiting for a return of his desire. And then, looking at her, and from her to the slightly crumpled pillowcase, to the edge of the sheet, he was struck by an idea, and he wrestled against it for one brief interval, knowing, it's all wrong, it is unimportant, you use it because you are afraid of failing her; but he could not help himself. His heart beat very fast when he said in a whisper: 'Are these fresh sheets?'

Catherine did not seem to think of any implication, and she answered seriously: 'Well, yes. Not of today, they'll change them on Wednesday.'

It was some time before he could go on. He seemed to be suffocating.

'You have been,' he finally uttered, 'you have been ... he has been lying on these same sheets then.'

There was a long silence.

'I'm sorry,' Catherine said. 'I didn't think of it. I'll have them changed tomorrow.'

*

There was a message from Ernst of Hollandia who had called to say that a land-duty letter for him had come there, and he went to the land office; he found, to his surprise, that he was not very upset by the idea. He felt worn out after all his storms, and he was living from hand to mouth, completely unable to find anyone who had a franc left for lending. The man at the office told him that all cases were treated identically – the term was two months for all foreign students without a resident's visa, he couldn't request more than a week's postponement, he could pick his own farmer if he informed them of his choice within three days He went to Wouter who had done this work the year before and had told him his farm was pleasant. Wouter was at home, puttering around in an old dressing-gown, and gave him the address of a farmer near Lucerne, about as close to Zurich as Anthoni would find one, he said. Anthoni telephoned the office from Wouter's place, and they approved the address.

'Sit down now,' Wouter said, 'and I'll make us some coffee.' He had a room in an ancient house, on one of the few green streets in Zurich, the windows were low over the ground, looking out on a neglected garden which reminded Anthoni of the illustrations in an old-fashioned novel. He gazed at the dry little fountain with its stone frog, and he thought, it's only half past eleven, in two hours everything was settled, I don't seem to have worried about it very much this time, leaving Zurich in

126

a few days. I will come back every week, of course, what would a ticket cost? What will Catherine say? Well, I couldn't have waited in Zurich illegally, and without a penny, I still do not have to go, I'll see Jean-Pierre first. It was as if he had gone through this already once, and the way of least resistance was now unavoidable.

At the foot of the fountain some weeds were sprouting, and among them grew small red flowers on long stems, hanging over and almost touching the ground. 'Do you drink it black?' he heard Wouter say behind him, and suddenly he saw those flowers against the grey stone with a breathtaking sharpness, and he seemed to know that he had lived this moment before in his life, the garden, the voice, leaving Catherine, and that it had ended bitterly. He felt a shock of fear which passed, quickly.

He went to her from there, and fell down on her couch with a wry smile, and said: 'Catherine, may I have lunch with you here?'

'Yes, of course, Toni,' she said, and put down her brushes. She bent over him and stroked his hair. 'What has happened?'

'Nothing much, it had to come about one way or the other. It was just a question of which would catch me first, the war or the bloody land duty. The land duty won. I have to go bring in the harvest next week.' His voice sank while he spoke, and his face changed. 'Oh damn it, damn it all,' he said 'I'm a bit sick right now of the world pulling at me. I'd like an ivory tower for a week or two, God, or a wooden one if necessary. Oh, you know, Cath,' he continued, 'it isn't so grim, I'll come to Zurich at least one day a week, and when I'm finally sure about leaving for England I'll return here right away of course, I can tell them then to go to hell – it helps my finances anyway, I was sort of getting shipwrecked – it's near Lucerne – it can't be more than an hour by train . . .'

'I'll come to see you, Toni, if you can't come here,' Catherine interrupted.

'Really, Cath? What a sweet thing to offer.'

Catherine regarded him. 'Didn't you think I would?' she asked. 'I need to see you too, you know.'

No, I didn't think that, Anthoni said to himself, I never expected that, what a foolish and lovely mistake I made, I thought she would not care much, no that is not it, I hoped she would care but I imagined that she would not bother, would not allow herself to be bothered, interrupted in her work, would see it as a natural ending to an episode. He took a deep breath, it was as if a crushing weight had been taken off him, everything would be all right, it was all a wild and not unhappy adventure.

*

Sunlight fell from behind his head and he knew again that he was in Catherine's place, that she had asked him to stay; he fell into a reverie, it had been such a tender night, a new gentleness had been in her, and in everything; it was a new sensation, waking up beside her in the late morning. It was Saturday.

'I have to get up immediately,' Catherine had said, 'I'm dying for the sun and the wind, can't we go somewhere?' He had taken her to the students' rowing-club at the lake, which had a landing-platform usable for sunbathing. He had counted on finding somebody there he knew to bring them in as guests.

The gate was closed and the place seemed deserted. 'I'll get us in somehow,' Anthoni said, and just then a Dutch student, Rolph, came out towards them along the path in the grass. 'Hello, Rolph, Miss Valois, you met,' he murmured, 'we want to sun, could you let us in?' 'You'll be here alone, but you should sign the book,' Rolph answered, 'and if nobody comes before you leave, be sure to close the door.'

'I have been in this place before,' Anthoni told her, and led her up the stairs in the boathouse to the dressing-room, which covered half the second floor and looked down on the boats. They changed, and he carried two deck chairs out on the mooring. It was an exceptional day, an intensity of blue all around them, in between the planks the water looked cool and dark, and the wake of the boats on the lake made the platform bob gently. He sat next to her, they held their eyes closed and felt the sun burning on their faces. There was a light breeze. They did not speak.

Catherine sighed, he moved his head sideways and looked at her, and then he said, 'you are very exciting in your bathing-suit, Cath.'

She smiled at him, and let her hand with her nails downwards glide lightly over his chest. 'So are you,' she answered.

They remained there almost motionless for a long time, the light white through their eyelids.

'I have to go home soon,' Catherine whispered. 'Yes, it is very hot,' Anthoni said.

Entering the dark boathouse they stood still, dizzily, and then he went up the rickety stairs ahead of her. She took off her bathing-suit, and closing her hands over her head looked at him with a smile. He did a hesitating step towards her, and stopped, and said: 'I must just look at you and admire you, Catherine, you are Aphrodite rising from the sea,' and he pressed her against him as hard as he could, longing for that pain.

'What can we do?' Catherine said. She trembled.

He was trembling too, he had never experienced this desire.

He shook his head. 'It's impossible,' he whispered, 'somebody might come in any minute.'

They dressed without speaking. The wave of wanting which had filled and overwhelmed him went, and left him cold and half sick. When they reached the door it was opened from the outside, and a member of the club entered, carrying a battered leather briefcase with a towel sticking out, who gave them a suspicious look.

They walked down the path and he closed the gate behind her, and then they stood on the wide Mythen Quay which was endless, deserted, and forbidding under the baking sun. 'I have to hurry home,' Catherine said. 'Yes, I'll take you to the stop,' he answered. 'The city is getting empty.'

He did not get into the streetcar with her. He had had a fleeting idea of asking her to come with him to his room first, but he did not.

He lifted his hand as a good-bye, and then he crossed over to the shadow of the trees and slowly walked towards town. He could see her streetcar for a long time. He thought of her body, as she had been standing in the half-light of the boat-house with her arms over her head, and he thought of her lover from Zug who was waiting for her.

*

Jean-Pierre had given up his apartment the day he went to Geneva, and he was now living in a downtown hotel, one block from Bahnhof street.

The door stood ajar and when Anthoni called out hello, he heard Day's voice shout from somewhere: 'Come in, who is it?'

'Anthoni,' Jean-Pierre said, 'I'll be damned, so you finally showed up. I have spent a fortune on phoning you, my friend, you have become the most elusive man of Zurich. Where have you been, what are you going to do?'

The place, he had a suite, was hot and in an indescribable chaos, clothes and magazines lying all around, a row of women's shoes stood at the door.

'I'm desperate,' Jean-Pierre continued in a half-serious, half-mocking tone, 'we are in a fix, I can tell you. Did you know that Lennard is under arrest?'

'No,' Anthoni cried.

'Yes, he and many more, the Swiss made a raid on the Gaullists; it was all planned, they are neutral you know, the Germans complained about the activities of the French here, and what do they do?' He paused and groaned. 'They arrest them, Toni, they have arrested nine out of ten, under some security of state clause, and they are being held incommunicado.'

Anthoni sat down. 'Jesus, what a blow,' he murmured.

Day seemed to find some relief in this dejection. 'Yes,' he

130

repeated, 'it's quite a blow. Oh well, the Maquis will manage without us,' he added.

'I guess the air supplies from England are being stepped up anyway,' Anthoni said.

'Yes, they'll manage,' Jean-Pierre answered, 'Money was the main thing you know, I mean the French francs which were brought to them from Switzerland.'

'But Switzerland was important as a hide-out, too.'

'There is one new way opened,' Jean-Pierre now said solemnly. 'You'll keep your mouth shut about it. We have a new passage near Vallorbe, and it is being used. Two escaped prisoners who had been condemned to death were smuggled to Switzerland this week.'

'How do you know all this, Jean-Pierre?' Anthoni asked wearily.

'I'm activated. You know who took over Lennard's work as far as possible? My father. And I am the man for Zurich. We are building up an enormous stock for them, and when this has blown over I'm taking it to France myself. And you can come with me,' he added.

'When?'

'Just keep in touch with me, Toni.'

'I'm supposed to go harvesting next week.'

'Well, you'll be able to come to Zurich, won't you? I'll give you a tentative date. Don't fall out of your chair. First of September.'

'September!' Anthoni said, 'but that is an endless time.' He walked to the washstand and let the water run over his hands, and dashed his face with it.

Day now appeared to be recovering his good spirits. He rang the service bell. 'Anthoni, we'll be in Paris before you know it,' he cried, 'you go harvesting a bit first, don't grumble, it's fine for the nerves. Your Catherine must be quite a strain on you, confess it. You'll come back here as good as new.'

A man appeared in the doorway and Day continued in the same gay voice: 'Ha, my friend, there you are, please take all these shoes and have them cleaned nicely,' and, addressing

Anthoni again, he rambled on: 'Claude has been staying with me, but she is moving today, she got her own room back. I can't say I'm sorry, she is a tiring woman. She talks a lot about you, Toni.'

Anthoni smiled sourly. A dozen diffused thoughts swirled through his head. With Day everything always seemed so simple and possible; Day would not dream of going on land duty; was he being a fool, should he stay?, he could sleep somewhere, first of September, two months of dodging the police. He looked down into the deep narrow alley between the hotel and the neighbouring house, a man carrying two garbage pails entered it from the dazzling sunlit street and halted, putting them down to wipe his head. Should I try and borrow five hundred francs from Jean-Pierre? Anthoni asked himself. He opened his mouth and closed it again. He leaned his forehead against the glass. 'Jean-Pierre,' he said, 'please lend me a hundred francs.'

*

That week-end the sky remained a hard Southern blue and a merciless heat hung in the streets. On Monday morning the weather was still unchanged. It was early when Anthoni went once more to the land-duty office. There was a hairdresser next door with a mirror in his window. I look incredible, he thought with a grim sort of satisfaction. He had stayed indoors reading all Sunday, he had slept heavily and his eyes were swollen, he had not shaved in two days. The collar of his shirt was torn. He had the vague feeling that the land-duty people would mark the change in his appearance and realize that it was their fault.

He sat down opposite the same man and stared up at a poster on which two bronzed students were helping a thin and pious-looking farmer with a burden of wheat. *Plan Wahlen*, it said on it in red lettering. He put the most intense expression of disgust on his face that he could muster, and hoped it was noticeable.

'Here is the train ticket,' the man said. 'The farmer will pay you ten francs fifty each week. We have a local inspector who calls about once a month; it is from him that you will recieve your return ticket.'

'Thanks for nothing,' Anthoni replied audibly, and taking the envelope he left, smiling at himself because of his childish words.

The woman of the Parade Square house stared at the stubble on his face while he told her that he was leaving the following day. He was not really thinking of what he said, it was a nice place, he thought, too nice even to call her a landlady. Why did all people who rented out rooms look so wicked? There was a communal expression of meanness on their faces.

'You should have given me a month's notice, sir,' she said.

'Ha,' Anthoni cried, 'you have the government to blame for that. They need me to provide you with your daily bread.'

There was a moment's silence

'As a matter of fact, I'd like to retain the room,' Anthoni continued on a sudden notion. 'I guess it would stay empty during the summer anyway.'

They agreed on twenty francs a month while he was away. He would be back on the first of September, he said.

Having decided on this he did not have to collect his belongings. He put some clothes in his smallest suitcase, stationery, books from the library; he shaved in a hurry, caught by the urge to get out, and he went down, taking the suitcase with him, he did not want to come back for it next day; he took the streetcar to the station for the books were heavy, and checked it at the luggage room. When he came out again he halted in the shadow of the roofing.

He had a sensation of freedom and looseness which lifted him. He started walking towards Catherine's house.

*

For a moment he stood still in front of her apartment door. This is it then, he thought, my last night, but there will be others, it's the last of a period only, the end of the beginning; and he tried to smile as he went in.

133

The picture Catherine had begun during the days she had stayed indoors with her cold was on the easel, almost finished. It was the side of a house, the wall covered the canvas entirely, black with a yellow light emerging from the one window. She stood up and looked at it with him. 'I'm going to call it The terrible house,' she said.

'I think it's a brilliant idea,' Anthoni murmured, 'it would have been so obvious to make it an old house with ivy and ghosts; the horror for me is the newness of it, fears living in apartments, not in ancient castles.'

Catherine looked at him with something like surprise.

'I know you think me a materialist,' Anthoni said, 'but I'm not, I don't believe that a shot of the proper hormones would have changed Dostoyevski into a police officer. I think the earth, and the universe, are cool and immense machines, but there is nothing sterile or poor in that, because behind, behind it . . .' He hesitated. 'I believe in a real mysticism,' he said, 'in a metaphysical one, that is, not in an earthly one.'

'You once told me that the fourth dimension did not exist.' Catherine answered.

'What, when did I say that? Oh, no, I only meant that you shouldn't fiddle around with mathematics – in science there are no vacant rooms for such things. I might have seemed contradictory, but I think I was arguing in reaction, against the questioning of what is true in formulas on paper anyway.'

'Tell me,' Catherine answered him, 'what were you going to say, about those machines of yours not being sterile?'

Anthoni smiled at her, there was a bit of a pose in this now. He said: 'Because behind it all, I think, is love.'

There was a silence. Catherine looked at him. 'What made you study physics, Toni?' she asked.

'Oh, I don't know,' Anthoni began in his hesitating manner. And when she continued to look at him, he went on: 'It's a basis, Cath, it's something like citizenship for a Roman, that wasn't a goal in itself I don't think, it was a foundation. You could stand on it and be free to do whatever you wanted. Now the earth was dark once, I mean it was without order, and then

134

they started discovering that it was as well ordered as the stars. You know about the man who dropped those things from the tower of Pisa.

'Well, anyway, he found that a leaf fluttering down and a stone falling both follow the same rules, that only seemingly is everything on earth varied and incidental. And knowing that, realizing that, seemed a platform to me, do you understand what I mean? Without physics you seem to fall back into the world of mystery out of which we once emerged...' He stopped: I'm repeating the words of long-ago ideas, he thought, these endless discussions, I told myself that Catherine cannot be wooed, yet that is what I try, to force a road into her self-sufficiency, since she gives me her body I seem out to win her mind.

'I don't know a thing about science,' Catherine only answered. 'Did you get stranded in it, Toni?'

'No, I'm not stranded, but right now it doesn't seem quite the thing to concentrate upon. It was disappointing, of course, specialization always is; I guess I'll manage to finish it, though. These students, with their little notebooks – when the professor picks up a piece of red chalk, you hear a hundred clicks – they are all turning on the red in their four-colour pencils. It makes you shiver.'

After a while Anthoni said: 'Catherine – could you ever marry me?'

'Can you quite visualize us in that role?' Catherine asked in an almost tender voice. 'I think it would be a catastrophe. I'm sure I would behave very badly '

I think you would, Anthoni thought, how extraordinary that I would want it, Catherine could drive me insane.

'What would you do the whole day?' she asked.

'I have never thought of that,' Anthoni replied in a light-hearted tone, 'I don't quite see myself as a physicist. I would like to bring in more money than you, but since that's sort of impossible there doesn't seem to be much point in adding a few francs.'

'Oh, but you know,' she said seriously, 'I'd pay for my

135

wardrobe and things like that, but never for the household.'

'We'll do it fifty-fifty,' Anthoni answered. He felt displeased with this conversation. There was something wrong in it. 'Play me some of your records, Cath,' he said. 'I still haven't heard them.'

Catherine stood up. 'I'm going to play Cleopatra five times,' she announced.

It was as if the colour, the mood of the room, changed in the music. She sat on the arm of his chair and let her feet dangle, he took her hand and held it for a moment against his lips. He looked at the reflection of the room in the window. How sad we will feel, he thought, when we play this record later, thirty years from now. Catherine will look at herself, the memory will be unbearable, the days, the precious time, youth, her beauty – this moment, this second, never returning; I will listen and think of her as she looks now, we will be old and so sad, and it can never come back, never in all time. He got up and went to the window and drew a C on the glass with his finger. He walked back and stood still in front of her, and something in his face made her get up, and he embraced her.

*

He woke up and the light in the room was still on; Catherine slept with a silent face. It took him a moment to remember the reason for the joy there was in his utter tiredness. I have made love to her so well, he thought, as never before, and she had me so completely. Our whole relation seemed different. The strength in me was augmented by its recognition in her, she was dominated and loved me, loved me because of that.

How can one ever understand the relationship between two people without knowing about their love making, which is never spoken of, a taboo?

Strange, it seems almost unfair that it is so vital. But that is as it should be, for it is not a physical happening, it is a deeper force; it was the invisible mood around us which created this night. Nothing to do with technique, it's not like tennis or something, it came from Catherine's passion, no, love – did she then love me, does she? Do I love her, since I can make love to her only when I feel her tenderness, feel that I am not alone? I must put out the light, he said to himself, but he fell asleep before he had turned around.

The weather had broken, the light entering through the flowery curtains was dull and the wind was whistling along the edges of the window sill; the yellow circle of the lamp, still burning on the night table, gave him a sad connotation with sick rooms. He stared at the ceiling, it had a wreath of sculptured flowers in the middle, unobtrusive under the plaster, his lips formed the word today, today, and of a sudden he pressed Catherine in his arms and fought against his tears. She woke up instantly and without asking anything stroked his hair, repeating, Anthoni, Anthoni. He forced himself to calm down and he managed to utter: 'I'm sorry, Cath, I don't know what is the matter with me, I know I will see you again in a few days, but somehow, it does seem like an ending, it makes me so sad . . .'

'I am honoured by your tears,' Catherine whispered.

It was such a miserable day, gusts of wind and rain from a wan sky. They walked to the station, it was close and the streetcars were packed. He got his bag and put it in a compartment of the train and then he stepped off again, and regarded her, looked at her eyes, how dark they were, he touched her hair, and then he turned around quickly and took his seat. He saw her head until she had vanished among the people along the platform, and he leaned back against the wooden partition and was without any thoughts or feelings; and then another man got on, and he sat up and held a newspaper in front of his face, blinking at the dancing letters.

*

The king riding out of Brussels at dark, where had he read that? The shortness of the life of one man in time – a passage

137

about a king, he did not know which one, leaving the town, galloping over the wet stones and then through the woods which came so close to it – in a far past, it was a year with fourteen hundred in it. He had never forgotten the sound of those words; he could not quite recall them now but he remembered sharply the emotion they had evoked in him. The Middle Ages, and then the idea of a rainy evening, so very long ago, and yet rain on streets in which he himself had walked, a wood that still was; he had seen it, that man riding out because he wanted to think alone, the drops falling softly from the leaves of the trees, oh how much that evening must have seemed the now to him, how tracelessly it had vanished. He could think about it without end, about those glittering silent streets and paths, the moon would have played such a part in that world of dark nights, the king looking up at it and seeing it follow him through the foliage; how to conceive of life then, an age of mystery, the ocean the border of the known, wolves in the woods around Brussels? Why this image through time, why a feeling of pity for that lonely man riding, halting to stop the sound of the hoofs and listen to nothing but the silence, the dripping of the rain, the beating of his heart, five hundred years ago?

*

The four-o'clock knock on the ceiling below his room aroused him and he put his clothes on without really opening his eyes and stumbled down the staircase and out into the light of the predawn morning. He was supposed to help rake grass, four men mowing, he with another man behind them; it was all done by hand and it seemed an incredible scene to Anthoni. The other helper had stepped out of a painting by Breughel, he thought, he had the face of a complete imbecile. His raking was more efficient than Anthoni's, and he usually did Anthoni's stretch over again. They never exchanged a word.

It seemed an endless time under the steadily brightening light, the sun rising behind the clouds, before they sat down and pulled out their bread boxes and Anthoni went into the house for his breakfast. He was considered a gentleman because a student, but as he was paid one fifty a day, probably not much less than what the worst-paid labourers received, his efforts were scrutinized by Iel, his farmer.

Iel seemed meaner and more stupid in reality than he had been in the stories of Wouter, who had given the impression that his land duty the year before had consisted mainly of cider parties with all hands present. Iel tried to spur him by putting the jobs to be done in an impersonal light, as if they were tasks imposed by some superhuman necessity and not undertaken to make money for him; but Anthoni's mind was so entirely occupied with other thoughts that most of this passed over him.

He could not however hold himself aloof physically, for he suffered from an ever growing weariness since he had to get up at four and could not go to sleep at eight in the evening like the others, and from a consciousness of time as he had never experienced. When he thought it was noon, it was nine in the morning, and his sense of time never got adjusted. A conception, faintly held, about the healthiness of it all, the elementary truths to be found in contact with the earth, had vanished immediately. The farm seemed a money-scraping institution, the labourers underpaid cretins who muttered and protested all day, the work a senseless toil because of the lack of machinery. From the beginning he focused all of his mind on Catherine, and on seeing her again, but it took him a long time before he learned to think during the hours of the day – at first their very endlessness had left his mind a blank, unable to grasp any thought.

This great war is yet only a war, he said to himself, I have to play a part in it, for the record, my own personally kept record, but surviving that, I will be at a beginning, life, which it is highly necessary to consider. For it seems to have so few attractions left, in itself. The idea of finishing my studies, undertaking work, is empty, and so I have kept telling myself, I won't have to, there'll be other ways.

And as my final refuge there was the nebulous voyage, the

dim decision to leave it all if that had to be, to go away, go under in the brightness of a Southern country, the light and the colours, and I would be free on all the earth and therewith free of the anxieties and the sorrows of the many, who bind themselves. This was before Cath. Catherine is my central point. My actions and my thoughts are not diffused, not parallel, they have become radii towards her. When I think of where to live, of money, of places, of clothes even, I think of her; what does this mean, did it come over me like a wave or did I conjure up the new pattern because I wanted it unconsciously? Oh, but that is to say, do I love her or do I want to love her . . .

But nobody knows whether love exists, he thought later, what it is, where it begins; love filling the universe, and human love part of that? Love is not-aloneness, and is to love somebody to be never alone any more, to become part of an immortal essence? I am philosophizing like a first-year student – I admit that I wanted to make love to Catherine for vain and trivial reasons, that is how it started, and her painting made her fascinating, and all her money, but that is not what love can be built of.

Death, the ending of I, was the ending of human loneliness .. and now, this day, it seems different to me. On this summer day, on this bloody cornfield, no matter the reasons I give, the trivial beginning, loneliness is separation from her. This is my love, or might be, and so her desire can become, too, love. For there is only love on last sight.

*

'I have such trouble,' he wrote her, 'arranging for time to come to Zurich; I told them that I didn't want Sunday off but a week-day, which stunned them. I could take a day this week, but could only leave after eight in the morning, which means in Zurich at ten or eleven, and then dirty, disorganized, and extremely sleepy – does it not seem better for me to come two days next week? Tell me what you think. It is a misery not to see you for at least another eight days; when I come I'll have to gaze upon you from morning till morning, but then there is your work and other things –'

He paused. He was sitting in his room at the window, writing on the sill, ducking moths which were flying in at the light; it was late evening and very still, the sky was black with no wind. He was deadly tired but there was a nervous excitement in him which had made him get up again; he had to talk to Catherine and writing her, having the sensation of communication, was the only thing that helped. He knew that a thought, a consolation, fluttered somewhere in his head, and in his weariness it took a conscious effort to get hold of it. Yes, that's what it was, use their separation for a restoring, for a sharpening of the edges. And write her about myself, about my ideas, my discovery of love; to conquer a place in her spirit – his thoughts dwelt for a moment on the classic correspondences of history.

'I desire you so, Catherine,' he wrote, 'and my desire is a directed one, it is like a magnetic force, vehement in one direction and zero in another, the first time I made love to you I was in love with woman, and as such a very inexperienced man I'm afraid. I am in love with you now, and my desire is for your body only, because it was born in your body only. And when the form this content takes is incomplete or weak, then that is because this feeling is not a taking but a giving, and so it needs the open door to bring the gift in, as you were open and accepting on our last night.'

He reread it and said to himself, there is something wrong with this, and I cannot lay my finger on it, are these just phrases? Should I simply tell her about the raking of the grass and the loading of wheat on carts, and the sun and the flies and lack of sleep, and should my love shine through that? A short story might be the ideal love letter, but then I should not try to be artistic . . .

'Dear Toni,' he read, 'I'm sending you a hasty note which Anne-Marie, who had lunch with me, will mail right away. My work has suffered a lot because I have been incredibly nauseated for some days. It is my own fault, and then it is not, for it has happened to me before, and my doctor tells me it is impossible to eliminate the risk completely. Anyway, what it comes down to is that I need a curettage. I feared it already last week but thought I might be mistaken. It's a bad thing, you know, no matter what they say, it is a blow to your body, and right now I'm thinking, I'm through with love for a year.

'I'm not too upset, my doctor knows what he is doing. I'm going to his house on Saturday and he will keep me there for two days, that's how he works this, otherwise there is a risk of complications. It's not such a small operation – it costs a lot of money too. I want to be back at work on Tuesday, but I'll take the week-end off, and I'll come to you. It seems unnecessary that you should do the travelling when you have so few hours. I think I'd like to go to Lucerne that Friday night, if I feel well, that is. The invasion seems at a standstill. Don't work too hard . . .'

*

On Friday Anthoni was in a state of extreme vexation. He had wanted to speak to the farmer at breakfast, but he had let the occasion slip by. I'll talk to him at noon, he thought. Here I am, the days have gone by and I'm only the worse for it. Rousseau, nature, meet Catherine again a new man, what stupidity; through ten centuries the best men and the best women have left the land and gone to the towns, and only those who were too dull remained behind to make their living by toying with dung from sunrise till sunset. No wonder they look at me and my books with stupor.

He tried to avoid each not absolutely necessary movement, whatever he did he had the feeling that it was energy wasted, that he would be that much less when with her.

'I have to leave at five,' he told Iel, 'the last train to Lucerne is at a quarter to six.'

'But that's impossible,' the farmer said, 'it's the best part of a day's work that I'd miss from you.'

142

'I just have to,' Anthoni answered; he felt so annoyed and so helpless in this wrangle with the man that he had to make an effort to keep himself in check. Next thing I'll start crying, he thought with disgust.

'The other hands wouldn't stand for it,' Iel continued. 'As it is, you do half of what they do, you're only thinking about books and letters and stamps.'

'I'm a student,' Anthoni said, 'I'm certainly doing more than my friend Wouter last year. He can't lift the queen of spades.'

As always Iel's face brightened when Wouter's name was mentioned.

'Yes, he wasn't very strong,' he admitted with an amused smile, 'but then, you know, I didn't pay him, you get a wage, and I have to pay the government for you too, and then there is your insurance, it mounts, it all mounts.'

Anthoni felt better now. 'I understand,' he said, 'we must do something about that. I see your point, we'll work out some sort of an arrangement, I'm sure. I'll leave at five then.'

'Will you be back on Sunday night in time to help me with the milk?'

'Yes, certainly,' Anthoni answered, adding. 'I'll try, anyway.'

*

In Lucerne the sun had not yet lost its height, and he hastened along the quay in an unpleasant awareness of his dishevelled appearance, entering the lobby of their hotel with a sigh of relief when he found it half dark and empty, like all big Swiss hotels then; the lonely clerk did not seem surprised by his strange aspect but Anthoni thought it necessary all the same to accost him in a thin and supercilious French. Miss Valois hadn't arrived yet, she had reserved a room for him.

He sat on a chair in the bathroom with his head cupped in his hands, and it took him a long time to find the energy for moving. At last he got into a bath, and shaved, and then went to the window of his room. It looked out on a wide paved court, and over the low building at the other side the sun shone in; he had been severely bitten by black flies and the heat of its rays made him shift uncomfortably. He drew the curtains and lay down.

He was awakened by Catherine coming in and putting on the light. He felt as if he had been beaten and he was half-sick from drowsiness. 'Hello, Catherine,' he said with a dry throat. 'I'm so happy to see you. Forgive me, I'm a complete wreck.'

'Don't get up,' she cried, 'I want to look at you.' She stood at the foot of the bed. 'Yes, you're worth coming to Lucerne for,' she went on with a laugh at him. 'But you've changed! Sit up, please.'

Anthoni complied a bit sheepishly.

'Your chest has broadened,' Catherine said.

'That's from dragging Iel's wheat around the whole day.'

'But I don't like it,' Catherine remarked with a definite voice, 'it's not your style, Toni. Your shoulders must go down slightly.' She drew a contour in the air with one finger.

'Don't worry, Cath,' Anthoni answered, 'I'll soon either quit or be buried in the cesspool. I don't think I've ever detested anything as much...' He checked himself, I mustn't exaggerate this, he thought suddenly, it seems so weak, doing a job which you loathe, I must tone down the humiliation ... 'I guess my sense of humour has evaporated,' he went on. 'Do you want to go out?'

'I want to come to bed with you.'

It was over very quickly, and then there seemed to be nothing left in him but an immense longing for sleep, I feel as if I'd been awake since the day I was born, he sighed, but he forced himself to keep his eyes open. He pushed the pillow against the wall and sat up in bed. 'Tell me about yourself, Catherine,' he said, 'how did you do without me? Your letter startled me, I'm very sorry, I had no idea ...'

'It is all right, Toni,' she replied slowly. 'It all went well.'

'Did you have pain, Cath?'

'Only a short while. I've had this before, you know. But I've

144

never been so sick. You must disagree violently with my system,' he added in her anecdotal voice.

'Would you never want a child?'

Catherine uttered an amused, horrified cry. 'Oh God, no,' she said, 'it would be my undoing, of my mind and of my body. And of my work. My nausea is half psychological.'

'Cath,' Anthoni began, 'Catherine, you're not sure, of course, that it's my fault ...' While he spoke those words a complicated thought flew through his head, this is like Zola, he thought, girl doesn't know who the father is, that's supposed to be the ultimate in sin and degradation, why does it seem so normal, why doesn't it touch Catherine?

She answered lightly: 'No, I'm sure it was you, Toni. I've had this with Hans, and I wasn't half that sick then.'

He stared silently at the opposite wall. When he looked at her she was lying face down, her arms stretched and her hands resting against the wall.

'Did it cost you very much money?'

'Five hundred francs, but it doesn't matter, it's my own responsibility,' Catherine said in the pillow.

'Who is the doctor?'

'I have never told anyone.'

There was a long pause and a shock went through Anthoni when Catherine put her hand on his body. 'Toni,' she said softly, 'you're terribly nervous. Don't think about all this. I understand it upsets you, but I can't change myself. This arrangement is not forever, when you come back from your war we'll do things differently – don't forget that I'm an artist, not a housewife, I have to live according to my own standards. I'm very much concerned, the last thing in the world I want to do is to hurt you.'

'Really, Cath?' he whispered, and taking out those words only, he repeated: 'We'll do things differently later. I love you so much, Cath. Do you love me?'

'I don't belong to you, Toni, if that's what you mean, I don't belong to anybody. That was the first thing you asked me, I often wondered what made you say those words, it's the best

145

question anyone ever put to me. I love many things about you, I love your body.' She stroked him and he sat there, still, his burning eyes now closed. 'Please kiss me,' she said.

*

Their next day, Saturday, was the most brilliant they had ever had together.

They had moved to her room which had two beds, and he had lain next to her, his arm around her, in a joyful dear closeness which lasted without a word being spoken, he had made love to her in a bright way and from there on he had lived in the consciousness: this is a golden day; not wondering what to say, what to do next, no exerting himself to be different, stronger, keener, but an unchecked pouring forth of thought and of a loving which was asked for by Catherine and taken in.

They walked out of the hotel, he did not notice anything or anyone, and came out on the boulevard, he held her hand as they wandered along the lake, and then later along the big buildings facing it at the other, the shadowy side. 'You look so very young this morning, Catherine,' he said. The reflection of the sunlight on the stones and on the water played over her face, and then was intercepted by one of the marble pillars which extended in a row parallel to the waterfront houses. Such an intensity, he thought, I feel so inspired, the earth is regarding us, I am its master for this moment – He said to her: 'I feel inspired.' 'Will you write me an ode?' she asked. 'I want to live you one,' Anthoni answered.

'I do not know what has come over me,' Catherine said later, 'I feel sweet, and that is one thing I have never done.'

'I do too,' Anthoni cried, 'and in a clear cool way, sweet in a Latin way. Not tearful and German. Not like young Werther ever dreamed of.'

'I never read him.'

'I'm so glad,' Anthoni replied, 'I think Goethe is a highly dislikeable creature, a German burgher pretending to be a Hellene.'

Catherine laughed and said: 'Perhaps those men have spoiled a lot for us, they have talked too much about uncomplicated joys and made them complicated. If there's one word I loathe, it's picturesque, and I think they made us loathe it.'

'Oh, I would have liked to meet you long ago. I would have liked to await you in a garden on a brooding summer night, and gaze at the lights of the house until I saw you come, flying down the wide stone steps, holding your ball dress up, and I would embrace you and we would forget everything, and then you would hear voices calling for you and you would run, but first you'd press a key into my hand and whisper, the old iron gate –'

'And someday we would go riding,' Catherine continued quickly, 'and at a shady spot in the woods I'd say, my foot hurts, and I would dismount and sit in the grass and you would bend over me with a worried look and suddenly I would laugh and throw my arms around your neck and pull you down next to me. And I would just throw my skirts over my head and let you make love to me that way, because it took hours to get out of those dresses. The horses would return to the house and everybody would think us lost, and we would walk home and sleep in a hayloft on the way.'

'And your father would be waiting for us at the gate with his pistol loaded.'

'Oh, I would jump in front of you, and then his heart would melt and he would take your hand with tears in his eyes. Why don't people make love any more in nature? It must be so lovely to look at the sky while you are being embraced. Why don't we?'

'There are too many people in the world now, and houses, and roads,' Anthoni said softly, 'you have to buy being-alone now. But I want to, one day, we must go somewhere far, and lie naked on a beach, all alone, a desert island . . .'

They went back when the sun was still over the roofs, her room was filled by warm light, and he made love to her so long and so deeply, as he had never known, and it went through his mind, I did not believe that such a feeling existed, I have read it and thought it fancied, I did not know there was room in me for the dimensions of this.

*

He woke up very early and felt at a loss with all the hours. He muttered, why didn't I sleep till twelve, and got up and walked soundlessly to the bathroom, and when he came back Catherine was lying on her side with her eyes wide open. 'What is that you're wearing?' she asked. 'Nothing, an old pair of shorts.' 'Blue is your colour,' she answered firmly, 'you look nice.' He said then that he wanted to get up because he felt emptiness in himself; he knew that he could not make love to her, and guessed from her manner, even from the way she held her head, that she expected him to; and he slouched in a chair, smiling at her hesitantly.

There are houses built over the water in that town, and in the evening their continuous façade with its interspersed yellow and black windows made them the setting of an old century; and he said, 'Nothing would have looked different here three hundred years ago.'

A café terrace at the night of an endless Sunday; we are almost parting again, Anthoni thought, and yet I can't but be relieved. Why was this day so long? Why had the hours passed in such a blank – because we have never been together so much time without pause? I knew in the morning that it was a fruitless day, I wish I could have lied, saying that I had to go back then.

He could finally look at himself with some irony. I felt unappreciated, he thought, I actually counted the number of times and said, but that's not so bad.

'I'm not going back tonight,' he told Catherine, 'it was a sterile day and I do need a few more hours of you. I'll leave at some ungodly hour in the morning.'

He put his hand in hers. Darkness was falling quickly now over the terrace.

'There is a rhythm in life,' Catherine answered in an undertone, 'and the day after the party when you think the wine or the lobster made you sick, it's just the ebb. We had our party yesterday, you know.'

'Oh, Catherine,' he began quickly, and then he had to breathe deeply, and he suddenly said, not knowing why, not thinking, not wanting anything but because the words spoke themselves: 'I have loved you since the beginning of time.'

She said gently: 'I love you too, Toni.'

Later a lamp went on, throwing out a spray of light, and the waiter came up to them. 'We're closing the terrace, sir.'

*

The telephone rang, and he hit his hand against a lamp when he tried to locate it before it would wake Catherine. 'Four thirty,' the operator said.

When he was dressed, Catherine was fast asleep. He hesitated a moment and then he just bent over her and kissed her on her forehead. She sighed deeply. He walked over to the mirror and wrote on it with soap, good morning, dearest, and thank you.

The brightness in the streets struck him and he told himself, of course, they've already been raking for an hour, and he shuddered, and went on to the station and got into the rickety little train with his thoughts halted because that way he was halting events and not yet ending the days with her. The train had only two cars, with the wooden benches lengthwise, facing each other. In the far corner a man was sitting in blue dungarees who said something to him in the local German. 'Oh, go to hell,' Anthoni murmured. And then a whistle was blown and they began to move, and he swallowed and thought bitterly, it is over then.

They squeaked along the uneven tracks between the houses and gained speed and rattled on over a dam, the fields on both sides invisible under the low fog banks.

He walked to the farm and when he entered they were eating

breakfast; he exchanged a muttered greeting with them, nobody speaking a word. It's inconceivable that it is me sitting here in this kitchen, facing a pot of fried potatoes, he thought, that that man is eyeing me askance because I wasn't here to rake his grass, I'm sure they did as well without me, they might ask something, they live an hour from a town and go there once a year, they laugh at my tie on a working day, but if they only knew, if they only dimly knew . . Ninety minutes ago I was in the same bed with Catherine, I could have touched her with just this small movement, touched her body. Why do some women, why does she, seem more than human, so clean, so inviolable, why is it difficult to think of her as having a cold, no, differently, as having to obey someone? Her beauty, her money?

There was a scraping of chairs. He looked around him without meeting anyone's eyes, he gulped his whole cup of cold coffee and held it in his mouth as he went out on the wet earth, the sun already a quarter over the horizon; and there was an image before his eyes of that Saturday, of their walking together along the sunny street, along the row of marble pillars.

*

A dark sultry day, and when he entered the house in the evening, his shirt rolled up like a towel and tied around his neck, in an utter bedraggledness which seemed to make him impregnable, Iel's wife said in a flat voice: 'There's someone waiting for you in the drawing-room.'

He opened the door, for a fleeting moment thinking, Catherine, but the idea was gone before he had placed his visitor, a member of Hollandia whom he had met only two or three times, who was sitting rather stiffly on the horsehair couch in the semidark, never-used room.

'Hello,' Anthoni said, 'how on earth did you get here? I'm sorry that they kept you waiting without saying a word to me.'

'I knew they wouldn't call you,' the man answered with a

smile, 'my grandfather was a farmer, they're alike all over the world, I think.'

'My farmer is strictly a case by himself,' Anthoni answered and sat down on the floor.

'Money and time,' the man began pensively, 'acquire a certain absoluteness for the man who has to toil with the earth –'

'Please,' Anthoni cried, 'no dirty words. Tell me the good news I'm sure you are bringing.'

'Yes, can we go and have a drink somewhere?'

They walked to the train stop which had collected some dingy shops and two little cafés around it, and sat down at the window in one, ordering a carafe of red wine.

'The point is,' the man said, 'that the attaché in Bern is not doing so well in getting the convoy for England ready.'

'Don't tell me,' Anthoni interrupted, 'that man has been torturing me for two years now.'

'Are you still putting your money on the Dutch legation then?'

'I have my own iron in the fire and I think I'll finally manage, but it will not be before the first of September,' Anthoni said.

'Now listen carefully. I came all the way to this hole because you seem to be the one man in Hollandia who is serious about this. I have thought of a plan. Yesterday I got a letter from Rome, written after its liberation, two weeks ago.'

'Impossible.'

'My dear friend, you just don't know about the ways and means of the Church. It's a cousin of mine, he is a scholar and a big man, a prelate, and he has given me the name of a Franciscan who is the Prior of a Swiss monastery near Locarno, and I am going there tomorrow. Do you get the idea? Rather than try France, one could get through occupied Italy and cross the lines north of Rome, into allied territory – hopping from one monastery to another, with letters of recommendation. Let me finish, I have it all worked out. That Franciscan is a Frenchman and I'm very sure he'll sympathize with the plan, and give us letters and clothes and all that; I don't know whether we should dress like friars, it seems a bit melo-dramatic but might be the best thing. The Italian monasteries are safe places, the Germans just don't have the time any more to bother much with them. With French and Latin we will find our way.'

'But I can't imagine a prelate, whatever that is exactly, arranging such a thing,' Anthoni said.

'He isn't arranging anything, he'll just close one eye. Our story is that we have a mission in Rome and that the Germans refused to let us through, so it had to be done illegally. Don't talk about the war. And I'll show you how to cross yourself before dinner. They still have lovely wines in those places, you know.'

'I'm highly flattered,' Anthoni said, 'but why don't you want to go alone?'

'For no reason except that I don't feel quite up to it. What do you think about it? If you say yes, I'll go to Locarno tomor-row and write you about my reception there.'

He agreed, the plan had a nice colour, it seemed a happy thing to put away in one's mind, play with, the feeling of having one more trump somewhere, he thought, not quite up my sleeve, rather floating high up in the air, the whole trip sounds too romantic, and somewhere inside I have the definite feeling that it will never come off. But then, one doesn't know —

That evening became a strange one; the man he hardly knew and himself, thrown together by a scheme of trekking south in Italy disguised as monks, it exhilarated them. They finished their wine and decided that the place bored them, they crossed the road and ordered another carafe in the café there. They did not talk much. Anthoni sang snatches of song and suddenly he said, in a cold frightened voice: 'There was a boulevard along the lake and there we walked, in the sunlight, and the pillars, the white marble alternating with the blue sky . . .'

They were both silent for a long time. When they had finished the wine they crossed back again and now they began a long conversation in which Anthoni was, he thought, very witty, and the man started to sing Latin for him, and when they went out again for the next carafe in the other café, there seemed to be a number of people standing in the road to watch them, with benevolent smiles on their faces he imagined, and he walked over to a child and handed it a franc which it accepted in dead silence. From then on things grew vaguer, until they came out and found that it was dark and still on the road.

'I have to get home,' Anthoni murmured, 'and what about you, there're no more trains?'

'I'll walk to the highway,' the man stated happily, 'I'm sure to get a lift there from an army truck.'

They thanked each other for a long time, and then Anthoni was stumbling along a path, and he missed his turn, and came out on a wide field covered knee-high with weeds, and wood all around, and it began to rain and to thunder.

It seemed hours to him that he plodded around there, quickly so soaked that the rain could not hurt him any more, and lightning flashing over his head. Then he saw a house and knocked, and a man appeared, holding a madly barking dog by its leash, who showed him the road to Iel.

Iel's door was barred, and it was a long time before a sour-looking maid came to unbolt it. He made it up to his room, and then he dropped his clothes in one single movement and fell on his bed.

*

Going through the dewed grass, dragging his rake behind him, the other helper addressed him. 'That's some job waiting for us,' he said, looking past him, 'They are going to put us on the potatoes.' 'Is that so bad?' Anthoni could not help asking. 'It breaks your back,' the man declared with a smile.

Anthoni shrugged his shoulders in annoyance and halted to let him pass. He bent and picked up two handfuls of the newly cut grass and brought them to his face, inhaling the smell and holding them against his skin. It has to stop, he said to himself, and the knowledge that he could stop it that very day was almost anticlimactic. There just isn't the money, he thought,

153

no, what nonsense; I'll make do for these few weeks, I have to go back, I'm losing Cath, and I'm losing myself, I'm becoming a subdued flybitten labourer, no sleep, cows dogs, people, what a waste – To the others' amazement he just remained there, standing still and leaning on his rake, rehearsing those thoughts over and over to fortify himself for the coming conversation.

He caught the farmer at the door. 'Could we talk business for a minute?' he said, and his voice was changed, he spoke like a casual visitor from the city, and Iel heard it and answered him as such. 'Of course,' he said, 'come into my office.'

Iel got out his notebook and then regarded Anthoni expectantly. 'You have almost six weeks to go,' he finally said, 'twenty-seven August is a Sunday.' 'Yes, but I have to leave,' Anthoni stated. 'I can't interrupt my own life any longer.'

'Can't blame you,' the farmer replied unexpectedly. 'I never thought much of this student plan. Farming is a profession too, you know, you must be born in it to be of some use.'

The arrangement they reached was disastrous but Anthoni did not hesitate a second. 'Of course, you won't pay me my wage when I'm gone,' he said, 'but you will still pay one fifty a day for me to the government, except for Sundays that is, and so I'll cost you, say six weeks, fifty-four francs. Well, I'll just reimburse you that money. I'll pay you, to make it a round sum, seventy-five francs.'

'Suits me fine,' Iel answered. 'I won't tell a soul. But what do I say when the inspector comes?'

'Tell him I had to go to the doctor in Zurich that day. If he's suspicious you must phone Hollandia to warn me, and I'll come back. Will you do that?'

Now that it was all settled the farmer was a different man; 'No hard feelings,' he mumbled, shaking Toni's hand, 'you must understand, I have to look after my interests, had to get my money's worth out of you ... I hope Wouter and you will come pay me a visit one day, when the new wine is in.' 'Yes, yes, of course,' Anthoni replied without listening. He had sixty francs left of his loan from Jean-Pierre. He gave Iel fifty and promised him a money order for the rest.

'I guess you want to leave right away,' Iel had said; and he had nodded, although he had himself unaccountably planned to finish the day's work.

And so he stood in the doorway and saw Iel join the others who got up with difficulty from the turned-over vats on which they had been sitting, picking their teeth after breakfast. There but for the grace of God go I, he said to himself, but he felt somewhat ashamed, all over, three weeks, and hadn't he made too much fuss about it?

He stepped out in the yard and looked at the sky and closing his eyes he thought, I'm free. He ran up to his room in the silent and abandoned house, and then went to shave at the pump, putting up his mirror against the pipe, and every now and again, a maid passed by, carrying buckets from the stable, and giving the spectacle a long look.

Packing his bag he saw from his window a cart approaching along the road. He threw everything in and ran to the gate. 'Give me a lift to the station?' he called.

He looked back until they reached the bend and the roof of the farmhouse disappeared behind the hedges. 'Good-bye,' he murmured, and he half lifted his hand to some men at work far out in the field but they did not see him.

*

He was going to buy a box of chocolates at the newsstand in the Lucerne station when he realized that he had misread the tag which did not say eighty centimes but eight francs. He was seized by some sort of alarm, everything around him was so solid, the stand with its fruits and pocket bottles of liqueurs, the woman who had waited for his choice and sat back frowningly with her paper, the businessmen with their umbrellas; a porter bending under a trunk almost bumped into him, and then just briefly the pale eyes of the man met his, and in that moment he saw with singular sharpness the features, the white drawn face of the man on which two traces of perspiration drew lines to his chin, and he thought, God, that man is doing that job, day after day, just to stay alive, for no other purpose than to eat. How possible it is to starve, here I am with a few francs, a mountain of debts, not a penny to expect, what am I going to do?

There was an hour's wait before the train for Zurich left, but it was standing at the platform and he sat down in the corner of his third-class compartment and put his legs up on the opposite bench. He was glad for the delay. 'I have to muster my thoughts,' he said Money – Iel must have his twenty-five francs first thing, otherwise he'll play me some trick. Then there's my room and food, and no loan from the consul who thinks I'm harvesting – I need at least three hundred, two fifty – and then going to places with Cath, heavens what a mess – and all the creditors I evaded by going farming. First of September I'm saved if Jean-Pierre is good for his word – but the police, suppose the pension registers me as returned? He found some comfort in the hopelessness of the situation; he could not make do, no matter how, so obviously somebody, something had to intervene and help him.

Then there is still the Italian chance, he thought. I wonder what that Franciscan in Locarno had to say? I should have had a letter by now, of course. I guess Iel will forward it if it still comes, but, my God, I didn't even ask him to –

Suppose that convoy gets into shape before September first, the consul would write to Iel, perhaps come to get me ... Oh, Catherine, you are my undoing – He said the word 'undoing' aloud, and he saw Catherine's face; how extraordinary, he thought, I could describe it, I've never had that with anybody's face. The image was so strong for a moment that he involuntarily put his feet on the ground and looked out at the empty platform. I am coming back because I have to see you. I have to have her, alone, that man, that man from Zug – he tried to imagine how the man looked, perhaps he was on this train, he would walk up to him in a tunnel .. Then he felt something like pity; he must suffer because of me, he thought, or doesn't he know; depravity; the bright young engineer, he might like the idea of others making love to the woman he had discovered. The long barred imagining of the man embracing Catherine. Why don't you go to hell, he thought, and his words were directed at her, why all this, why am I not on my way to the allied lines? But I must behave, Cath didn't ask me to return, to stay in Switzerland. If I blame her, everything will be spoiled. There is nothing wrong with being ruined by a woman, it is a good fate. That man who sat on the window sill all night, in Balzac, he died of pneumonia saving the honour of his mistress, I thought it foolish, why didn't he take a chance and jump, or why not go back in the room, one could always run away forever, to America, you only live once, but now I understand better, he must have enjoyed it, enjoyed his death on the window sill, which made him immortal.

While his thoughts went thus, there remained in him an awareness of something unpleasant. Jealous, I'm jealous, he said to himself in a mocking voice. A woman is not a possession, nobody should have the exclusive rights, I have always thought that so primitive, the lord and master and all that barbarous to-do about virginity, taboos from the past.

But then I did not know, one cannot know about the pain. Why is it supposed to be funny when a man is deceived?, how I understand now, the man who prefers not to know, he isn't ridiculous, he is desperate. God help me, how can I ever make love to her again, I'll see the shadow of the man from Zug ... He drew his breath in sharply, almost crying out, for a violent shock had gone through his body.

He made a sound of contempt at himself The train had started rolling.

When he stood on Station Square in Zurich, Anthoni felt for a moment so relieved that he wanted to touch the ground and did so, pretending to tie his shoe. I feel like a starving man, he said to himself, I want to drink in the streets, the hard stones under my feet, the sounds of voices and music.

He took the streetcar up to Hollandia, and sat in the garden. He shifted his chair so that his face caught whatever sun came through the leaves of its one tree which had been pruned because it darkened the windows too much; there was no one there except Ernst who had remarked, 'Anthoni, you are terribly pale, you don't look at all like a farmer.' He needed money before he could go and reoccupy his Parade Square room, and more than that: he could not quite yet face the consequences of his return, and while in that little garden he was as in a resting place between two stages. He had not even telephoned Catherine.

I am afraid, he thought, for if I am ready to lose Catherine I will keep her, and if it is my life to keep her, I might lose her.

He sighed, and said to himself, come on, there are graver things in the world than this, try and be bohemian. The thought did not help, but sounded false, and in that instant he felt as he never had before, he felt trapped But there is really no way out for me, it went through his head dimly, she will not permit me seriousness, and I have become utterly unable to be casual and light. It was a deadly thought and he shook it off, and went inside.

At five o'clock he went to Catherine. The fact that she did not know he was in town gave him some dark uneasiness about whether she would be alone, but he left it at that. When he knocked at the door he heard her voice call out in German, a cool, perhaps annoyed tone: 'Who is it?' He swallowed and then without answering opened the door. Catherine was at her easel, working with a tired tense expression. 'Toni,' she exclaimed, continuing to paint for a moment, 'did you manage to get away again, how nice, why didn't I know?'

'May I sit down?' he said hoarsely, and sat on the couch. 'I've come back for good, Catherine.' He was not even aware of the fact that he had forgotten about the war and his pending departure, and she was not either.

'For good?' she asked, 'but how is that possible?'

'Corruption. I bought my freedom. It ruined me,' he could not help adding, 'but I had to.'

'Oh, Anthoni,' Catherine said, 'I do hope you haven't done something foolish for my sake ... I mean, I wish I could give you more, of myself, of my time ...'

'You certainly display more amazement than joy at my reappearance,' Anthoni murmured stiffly.

She looked at him in silence 'Oh, my dear,' she answered gently, 'but you've only been gone for two weeks, you know, you shouldn't have been so miserable about it.'

'Three weeks,' Anthoni said, fighting against a sensation of inimicality towards her. And then abruptly he jumped up and went over to her. 'Cath,' he whispered, 'I'm sorry. You are so very beautiful, I just want to be your slave.'

'Don't love me too much,' she began, but stopped and smiling, pulled his face towards her, and he kissed her on her eyes. 'Please celebrate my deliverance with me tonight,' he said.

*

Ellis and Ingeborg were drinking tea from plastic cups amidst bags and trunks when he came in, and they looked at him with so much surprise that he became embarrassed. 'I'm not a ghost,' he said.

'Anthoni,' Ingeborg replied with heavy emphasis on his name, 'but when did you get back to Zurich? Why didn't you answer our letter? Why do you look so worn out?'

He sat down on the arm of her chair and said: 'I came back two days ago – but tell me first, how have you been?'

'Ascona is a heavenly place,' Robert answered, 'we have decided to stay, at least half a year, and we're going back there tomorrow. We're here to pack ...'

'I'm so glad you came today,' Ingeborg interrupted.

'Leaving tomorrow,' Anthoni repeated, and he felt sorry

that he had neglected them, forgotten to answer their notes, so many times he had thought, Ingeborg is alone, I should go and cheer her up; and now they were leaving. 'How sad,' he continued, 'if I'd known ... when I got your letter I had already made up my mind to desert my farm, and I thought, I'll see you soon. My last weeks have been such a turmoil, children, it's not very interesting, but I'll tell you all about it that you care to hear. I know your farm theories, Robert, but please believe that this was different. I just had to get out, it was the damndest place you've ever not seen; I made a deal with the farmer and he'll cover me. I was not much use anyway. Now I'm back here, and illegally, of course, the consul doesn't know.'

'And when is the big day?' Ellis asked him.

Anthoni was silent for a moment. God, he thought, I actually did not know what he meant.

He blushed deeply as he said: 'My departure on the first of September with Day is a sure thing, but I'm also working on a wilder plan which is to go through Italy.'

'But Robbie should be able to help you with that.'

'Of course,' Ellis said.

He told them about the project of the man with the cousin in Rome without mentioning that he still hadn't heard from him, which must mean that it was not going to work and that the prior in Locarno had refused for some reason.

Ellis reflected on his words, and then he said gravely: 'It's very tricky, Anthoni, but I think it can be done if those church people really cooperate. I know that part of Italy by heart, I might even think of some reliable helpers for you.'

'Robert,' Anthoni exclaimed, 'you've changed. You used to call me a fool, and now you look as if you'd like to go yourself.'

'It almost seems as if you two had reversed roles,' Ingeborg suddenly said.

Anthoni reddened again. 'I would be grateful if we could have a conference with the Hollandia man,' he said, 'but I don't think he's back in town and you're so busy today. You know, if and when we go, we'd start out from Locarno and

160

could come to you first.' This is sheer nonsense, he thought, the whole plan is obviously off I haven't even tried to locate the man. But why should I? No need to worry, September one, that is solid – I need a piece of time here anyway, it is essential.

'Of course, of course,' Ellis answered him in a rather distracted voice. The interested expression had vanished from his face. He regarded Anthoni with something like concern and then got up and said, 'Toni, would you mind giving me a hand with a trunk I can't get closed. I'd rather not leave it to the movers?' Ingeborg looked at him and was going to make some remark, but she changed her mind.

When they were in the other room together. Ellis sat down on a bed. 'Listen, Toni,' he said, 'your affairs are your own, but you must remember that we are your friends. We aren't such fools, you know, we both realize that there's something wrong with you. Just let me know if I can help you in any way. You're not sick, are you?'

Anthoni answered: 'Thanks for what you said, Robert, you're very kind.'

'That is no answer. What is the matter? You know, I may have argued too much with you about this war, you shouldn't have the impression that I am a half-baked fascist or that I'm indifferent as to how it's going to turn out – I may have overdone my objectiveness.'

'That isn't it at all. And please don't think my intensity was a pose. This is still the just war for me, anyway the necessary one, the do or die one, I'll go there, I know I will. It's that . . . it is . . . it's so difficult to say, I'm less simple. I realize now that one can suffer as much in one's own little room as in a concentration camp . . .'

'Anyway,' Ellis said after a long pause, 'you're welcome in Ascona, always and for as long as you care to stay.'

'Thank you so much, Robert,' Anthoni replied, and he deliberated quickly, should I ask him, it's such bad taste, but who else is there, he would not mind, three hundred francs would save me. He could not refuse now; no, for that very reason I can't ask him.

And as they went back to Ingeborg, Anthoni felt annoyed with himself and even more with Ellis, absurdly, because he had not asked him for the money.

He offered to help them with their packing and cleaning, and at half past two Ingeborg fell in a chair and declared that she couldn't move another fork. 'Robbie,' she suddenly said, 'I want to go to a movie, it's my last chance for such a long time.' Robert frowned. 'Ascona has a cinema,' he said stoutly. 'Oh, don't be difficult,' she answered, 'I don't particularly want to see ten-year-old German musicals, and there are some films in Zurich which I should not miss.'

'I'll stay and help finish,' Anthoni told them.

'But I want you to come with me,' Ingeborg said.

'Yes, you go too, Toni, when the movers come this place will be crowded anyway. I'll manage from here on.'

'Well,' Anthoni began, but Ingeborg interrupted him. 'Please come,' she said, 'it is our last movie, that's an occasion you know.'

On the street he asked her: 'Which one do you have to see most, Ingeborg?'

'Oh, there are several on my list,' she answered in a vague voice, 'it was more the necessity of seeing a film on my last day. I like Ascona, but I miss the city – down there Zurich seems a city. I thought you and I should go just once more, we won't again for a long time.'

Anthoni pressed her hand. 'No,' he said, 'heaven knows, perhaps never, no, we'll meet again some day – dear Ingeborg, do you remember the first time?'

'Rosalind Russell in – what was it?'

'One of those disgusting pseudo-naughty things.'

'Oh, yes, no, I like her.'

'Anyway, I hope everthing works out all right for you two down there, it seems the perfect place for you to get all that messy past out of your system. Don't worry about Hollywood, when this war is finally done Robert will be ready to get out of this country too.'

'No, he won't, Toni. He likes it here, he is not going to budge. But I can't give in either, I have to try film again – I wasn't meant to live like a contented cat.'

'I wish I were one. A fat sleepy Cheshire cat, a wonderful life, Ingeborg,' Anthoni said.

'What is going on with you, Toni?' she asked. 'Are you in love?'

Anthoni muttered an indistinct answer.

'It's yes then,' she persisted.

'Yes.'

They took a streetcar downtown without speaking much, and when he followed her into the theatre he saw announced: *Shall We Dance*, and as they were seated he remembered the film. 'Ingeborg, what a nice idea,' he said, 'that was one of my favourites, long ago, I must have been twelve; oh, it's the one film I would want to see now. Why do they never make these happy simple pictures any more?'

She looked pleased. 'I thought you wouldn't mind if you'd seen it,' she replied. 'I wanted to go because I've never seen any of their films, I was in Germany then, of course.'

'You were too young,' Anthoni said with a smile at her.

'Then so were you,' she answered. 'I'm older than you, I'm afraid.'

'You're not. Anyway, I was a precocious child.'

A cartoon began, and he watched her profile while she looked at the screen.

'Who is she, Toni?' she asked, without turning her head towards him.

'A Swiss girl, French-Swiss that is, woman, I guess I should say,' Anthoni replied in a faltering voice.

'Is she beautiful? Why have you never told us about it?'

'It's, it is a strange thing ... it is a very complex affair ...' Why did I never even think of doing that, he thought, but then they would not go together at all, Cath is too, what? too special.

Ingeborg turned her head to him, closing her eyes a second

as if to reassure him. He suddenly started speaking rapidly, some words were lost. 'It is all so wild, you know, so unhappy and yet so happy; when it began it was clear to me, a woman who let me make love to her, it was uncomplicated, I mean – she was very beautiful, I had never seen, that is to say, she was exactly my type, that's such a stupid word, forgive me – she has grey eyes and, her figure is sort of perfect, she is very intelligent, so bright and yet so passionate, a cold flame ...' He checked himself, and said: 'Anyhow, Ingeborg, a man needs a woman and vice versa, don't you think, I don't mean it so crudely; I was having an adventure and did not want anything else – and then in a flash it all changed, I can't quite comprehend now how it happened and when and why – do you think I fell in love with love? I had a sense of recognition, she is my star, I thought, all stupid songs suddenly seemed of a profound philosophy, I yearn for her, my body but my heart too, I understand everything; it's a metamorphosis, my own living is not primary any more, I lost my instinct of self-preservation. Making love is dying, I would not mind dying like that ...'

'Since when all this, Toni?' Ingeborg asked.

'Just now, these days, being away. Oh, don't think I'm altogether crazy, I had insights of this, I had moments when I knew already where I was going.'

'Perhaps,' she said, 'you are having that emotion which is never shared, never mutual.'

'How did you come to say that, Ingeborg?'

'She doesn't love you, does she?'

Anthoni was silent.

'Not like that anyway,' Ingeborg said, 'don't you see, if she did you would have begun to feel less vehement.'

'I'm sorry,' Anthoni answered her without fully knowing why.

'For what, Toni?'

'For speaking so much about this, too much perhaps ... For what might have been and happened not to be,' he added in a tone more tender than she had ever heard from her. 'Don't be

164

too cynical about love, Ingeborg, it's not built on denial only.'

'I believe in it so much,' she said, 'that I won't even say now: don't get hurt.'

*

He was to see Catherine in the evening but at one in the afternoon, the morning finally behind him, the hours ahead stretched out so long that he decided to telephone her. He had reflected so much on the dangers of doing that that he felt only relieved when the girl told him she was not in. He did not leave any message.

For some reason the coming seven hours were now less difficult to pass. He was grateful for the emptiness of the summer city through which he could slum, as he called it to himself, and for the bad weather. One third of the summer is over, he thought, literally that is, but it really starts in May, in five weeks it will be autumn, September ... it seems to me as if I only have to survive this summer, as if the autumn will bring the solution to all problems. I think Jean-Pierre will keep his promise, but that's not it, I have an association of misery with sun in the streets, and the first fall evening will be so lovely, the lights reflecting in the rainy asphalt; September is my favourite month of course, it's Cath's too, she assumed it was because she was begotten in September, I hope I didn't laugh at that, it wasn't just cleverness of her, you must love life very truly to believe such a thing –

Catherine was wearing a green velvet dress and she was sitting in a deep chair, her legs crossed, reading under the standing-lamp which was the only light in the room.

He stopped in the doorway and she smiled

'I have to look at you,' he said, 'you are so dreamlike sitting there and so untouchable.'

'Kiss me,' Catherine answered, 'and make us a drink, if you please.'

When he sat opposite her he did not quite know what to say. He started three sentences and thought the better of them. He shouldn't tell about his slummed-away day, nor about the departure of Ellis and Ingeborg. 'I wish you'd come to Ticino with me for a week or so,' he suddenly said.

'I'd like to, Toni, but I can't I don't want to interrupt my work, I am hoping for an exhibition in spring. One of these days the owner of the Lavé is coming to have a look at my work.'

Ticino, he thought, I wouldn't have the faintest idea how to pay for that, but I would have found some way; it would have been the very answer – how discouraging that such a small thing could make so much difference. 'Is that the only reason, Cath?' he asked.

'Yes, Toni. You don't know how hard I work. I never seem to leave this room any more.'

'Did you do a lot today?' he asked with a slight tension in his voice.

She did not notice it. 'I made at least ten drawings. I haven't been out of the room and yet I didn't get tired. Do you want another drink? This is going to be a party, I deserve it.'

'No, thank you,' Anthoni said with a tremor, 'I guess I should go home early.'

Catherine regarded him with amazement. 'But you've just come,' she began, and added in a changed tone: 'Of course, if you have to, it can't be helped.'

Anthoni did not reply.

'I phoned you at one,' he suddenly blurted out, 'and you weren't home.'

Catherine put her drink down and stared at him for a silent moment, and said coldly; 'I'm tired too. If you want to go home I'll go to bed.'

He got up with a drawn face, and took a step, and when he was next to her he kneeled beside her. 'Forgive me, Cath,' he asked in a very soft voice, 'I'm such a fool, I am not like this at all, it's only an uncertainty, a transient thing, it has many causes, the waiting, the war –'

'You mustn't do it, Toni. I can't afford to be involved – I'm not worth so much concentration,' Catherine said, smiling again, and she stroked his hair.

166

'Worth?' Anthoni repeated, and the tension vanished from his face. He put his head in her lap. 'Oh, Catherine, I love you so,' he murmured.

Later he talked for a long time about England and the war, he again felt within himself the old excitement about the 'battle of light against darkness'; and he experienced a wild nostalgia for the time when nothing else in the world had existed for him, and he had an urge to make Catherine feel that way about it all, if only for a moment. He spoke with a nervous rapidity, there was a pain behind his eyes and he felt his face glowing. 'You're not listening, Cath,' he cried. 'I am thinking what a beautiful man you are,' she replied, and stood up.

He remained leaning against the door while she undressed. Life is so short, he said to himself, what does it all matter, I want to be in the here and now, I want to feel her body and mine, the joy of that, my hands, her face, they are too perishable. He came to her, thinking of himself, and then when he was very close he tried to direct his mind to other things so that he would be able to wait for her, and he did.

She lay on his arm in the dark and said, 'Will you tell me a story,' and he thought, and answered, 'I don't know any tonight, Catherine, next time I will,' and then later he whispered: 'Cath, I have to ask, but if you don't answer I won't again ... but if you want to ... tell me where you were today?'

'I told the maid I was at home to nobody. I was painting, Anthoni.'

*

'The bridgehead is absolutely secured,' Day said, 'and that's the one important thing. I've heard rumours that there will also be a landing in the south of France, the original Churchill plan. But no matter what, the war is won. These V-planes are only the final barbarity of the Germans.'

167

'I believe that they have no strategic meaning,' Anthoni muttered, 'it's that they seem so much more horrid than bombs from real planes with people in them . . . Tell me whether it's still Christmas in Paris for us.'

'The very thing,' Jean-Pierre answered, 'first of September was our deadline, and it remains that. Can you keep your head above water till then, Toni? Do you need another hundred francs?'

'Could you lend me two hundred?' Anthoni asked with an embarrassed expression on his face. 'I will pay you back, I'm in a mess, I've already sold everything I own and a few things I don't.'

Day started to look distractedly for his wallet. 'Listen,' he then said, interrupting his search, 'I sympathized with your feeling that you shouldn't go to Geneva until we were sure it would work . . .'

'You invited me to do otherwise.'

'I was jealous.' Day laughed, and Anthoni was not certain whether he was joking or not. 'Well, you were right. When a man is in too much of a hurry to run to the wars, my friend, it just means that first of all he doesn't know where he's going and secondly that his service isn't something to rank very high. Neither of the two holds for you.'

Anthoni bowed without a smile.

'Now, however, Toni, I find you changed. In fact I find you so changed that I'd say , this man has to leave, the sooner the better. For the first time I begin to worry about your waiting.'

Anthoni shrugged. 'I gather that emotions have gone out of fashion,' he answered. 'Everybody looks at me as if I had the whooping-cough or something.'

'Your diagnosis is not so bad. You do need a change of air.'

'You make me wince,' Anthoni said. 'I appreciate your concern. I can tell you that I did hope for a shot of that special humour of yours when I came to see you, God knows I need

168

it. But I'm in love, Jean-Pierre, I'm loving a unique woman, for better and for worse. I'm not a schoolboy enamoured of the chambermaid.'

Day regarded him very soberly now. 'When you made love to Catherine,' he said pensively, 'I did envy you, or rather, I was astonished at your quick success. I must admit that. Not that you aren't an attractive man. Now the deal seems less enviable, you are putting all of you on the scales, and your charming friend only her sex.'

Anthoni stood up and went to the window. 'I'm not amused,' he said.

'I don't understand your culture,' he then went on in an unfriendly voice, 'you wouldn't think it strange at all for somebody to go to a brothel, catch a syph, and ruin his life. He would just remain one of the boys; but a man who endangers his well-being for the sake of love, love, love, is considered a child or an idiot who needs a talking-to.'

'Of course,' Day answered calmly, 'since the first man couldn't help his misfortune, while the second one actually enjoys his.'

Anthoni smiled at Jean-Pierre and put his hand on his shoulder. 'You're quite right,' he said. 'I wouldn't want it otherwise.'

*

He went through the silent Sunday streets of late July, how barren the heat of the sun seemed in the city, how dark the brilliance could be. Gloomy Sunday, that was a song somewhere, who told me the story, it was banned because it made people kill themselves; if there are statistics about suicide days I am certain that Sunday is the peak, if you're happy it is a good day and Monday a bad one, but if you are at a loss with yourself it is the other way around; oh, if you're really unhappy it can't make much difference what day it is, what time, what season. How nostalgic a dead man would be for a day in spring – or for a day like this.

Zurich, a still town in this stormy summer. He walked to the station and past it along the Sihl river until he came to the water that was once the moat, and he followed it. It's at least better now than a hundred years ago, how stifling this dismal little town must have been on the day of the Lord in whom nobody by then was really very interested any more, how they must have puffed in their tailcoats, coming home from church, unbuttoning for an enormous dinner . . .

He stopped and turned around, and then went right. It was Tal street he had entered, and he proceeded with deliberate steps; he crossed Pelikan street and he halted past the corner, leaning against the wall of the houses and facing the windows of her place. He now began to lose his collectedness, and his heart beat in his throat. He made a grimace. There it is, he closed one and imagined a straight line emerging from the other eye, piercing the stone, the wood, like the dotted trace of a bullet on a picture of murder, entering the ceiling obliquely, and coming out in her room. 'Sunday afternoon, where can we go?' Hans said. 'There's really nothing, let's stay here.' Perhaps they had had luncheon in bed, he had made love to her and then they had a nap, they would go out for cocktails – but what difference does it make, why do I care, God, he certainly can't mean much to Catherine.

He started, he thought that he had seen the front door move. It was not so. I have never met her on the street, he realized, it seems impossible somehow that I would. Maybe I should have gone to her parents with her that week-end; it is inconceivable now, it is too late. A solitary man appeared at the far end of the street, approaching slowly He bent to tie his shoe, but when he looked up the man was still a block away. He is gazing at me, what does he want? Anthoni walked up to the next door and started studying the name plates, turning his back to the street, and waiting the endless minute in which the man's steps became audible, passed him, and vanished. There was a sudden emotion of mortal bitterness in him. He walked on and turned at the corner without looking back.

*

'The consul is not in town,' the girl answered. 'Do you want to speak to the chancellor?'

'Not in town?' Anthoni asked staccato, 'that seems odd, I'm glad he has so much time to spare. Yes, I'll see the chancellor.'

'I'm on leave for one day,' Anthoni told him, a kind and rather hazy old man. 'I used it to come to Zurich and discuss the convoy to England. That farm work is killing, I certainly wouldn't have used my free day for this if I could have guessed that the consul would be on vacation.' He was so indignant about the consul's absence at that critical time that he almost believed his own story and felt as if he had indeed sacrificed one day's leave.

The chancellor looked concerned. 'A regrettable coincidence,' he said, 'but perhaps you can still enjoy some of your day? I'm afraid I don't know much about the progress the convoy work is making; you can be assured that he will not let you wait longer than necessary'

'I can make my own arrangements,' Anthoni answered recklessly. 'But I need a hundred francs to tide me over.'

'Well, we should certainly – but you would have to wait for his return. He will be back before the first of September.'

'The first of September,' Anthoni exclaimed, 'but that's too much – perhaps he would rather have me go enlist at the German embassy – I'm sure they wouldn't keep me waiting.'

'I realize how you feel,' the man said, 'but such rash statements don't serve any purpose.'

'I'm sorry,' Anthoni replied and left the room. He felt a hard defiance within himself, thrown back again on the need to do something about his relationship with Catherine. 'May I use your telephone, please?' he asked the girl in the anteroom, and he called Catherine.

'Cath, I want to have lunch with you,' he told her, 'could we arrange that for this once?'

There was a moment of silence in which he suddenly felt the blood drain out of his face. 'All right, Toni, she then said, 'you can come and get me here.'

He took her to Huguenin and when Catherine said that she didn't want a drink because she had to work later, he ordered sherry for himself, and an elegant lunch. He emptied his glass and ordered another, and saw that these acts of rashness did not strike her as such. He forced himself to calm down.

'I dreamed of you,' he said. 'You were nude, and dancing for me.'

'Were my scars garlanded?' Catherine asked.

He frowned and shook his head at her, and looked over his shoulder at the waitresses.

'I hope you're not in a hurry,' he muttered, 'they're so slow here.'

'How is our old friend and enemy Day?' Catherine said after a moment, and her effort to speak about something neutral with him was worse than the most cruel remark, he thought. What is happening, we should have so many common things? 'Catherine,' he began, 'do you think we would be better friends if we had never made love?'

Catherine reflected. 'No,' she replied, 'I don't believe in the possibility of friendship without sex.'

'But, of course, there is such a thing as a spiritual friendship.'

'It's a sublimation then . . .'

'But suppose you met an old man whose ideas on art would mean a revolution to you?' Anthoni continued

'I would certainly let such a man make love to me,' Catherine answered with a laugh, without taking her eyes off her plate.

Anthoni did not pursue his thought. He waited until she was drinking her coffee, he put his hand on the table and she laid hers on his. Then he said: 'I want to ask you a question but for no roundabout reasons, simply because I have to know.'

'I know what you are going to ask,' she replied, 'and I will tell you, although you should know already. I am not in love with Hans. I wonder if I have ever been.' She stopped in thought. 'It's a relationship which will find its natural ending some day. He has done a lot for me.'

'One doesn't make love out of charity,' Anthoni said.

'But perhaps I like to, Toni. I'm a very demanding woman.'

Anthoni shivered. 'Listen, Cath,' he said quickly, 'I do mean something to you; I mean I can assume that and go on from there, I know that I can give you all you want – I can, in all the senses of those words ... but not now, not like this, can't you understand? I can't make love to you in that shadow.'

'The shadow exists in your mind only, Toni. When I'm with you I don't think of anything else. I wouldn't dream of questioning you about the time you're not with me. Do you want me to wait for you all day behind a barred window, like a Spanish señorita?'

'It seems a lovely idea,' he answered.

'I have to go back,' Catherine said. 'I'd like you to take me home if you still have some time. Thank you for a nice lunch.'

'Oh Cath,' Anthoni replied, thinking that the luncheon, the conversation, the not-to-be-repeated interruption of her work by him, should not be all in vain, should lead to a conclusion. 'I do want to talk this out, not now, just tell me that I may sometime?'

'Yes, Toni, you may. But you would make me happy if you didn't have to.'

*

I am going to my favourite place, he thought, it did bring me luck to write my letters there. He went to the terrace of the café at the Limmat, the days are shortening again, the sun is behind the tower of the Fraumünster, he said to himself. For a moment he considered his money and the ruinous lunch, two sherries, then he dismissed that.

'Dearest,' he wrote, 'since you had to go back to your work my day is but waiting to see you again, and I want to talk to you. A letter is a tricky instrument, written in one mood, read in another, and unless it is so strong that it carries its own mood with it and evokes it in you, it must fall flat – such a

173

warm idea, this piece of paper and the roundabout way it will take to reach your hand; I have the feeling that I could fly over Zurich and watch it with x-ray eyes along its route. I would paint that if I were a surrealist, and could paint. You would see through a roof a man lying dead in his room, and you would see a letter in a mailbox, and through another roof a woman at a party, everything else in the town would be vague, those three points only sharp.'

He closed his eyes and he did see this image, 'The Letter,' he said, and then he crossed out the sentence.

'Cath,' he continued, 'it is such a long way from understanding to acting what is called reasonably. For me there seems to be no way from the one to the other. I know what you want and what you want to give, and it is clear and fair. Yet it might not be the best thing, which can only mean: the thing which makes you happiest; and the man who did not go through the forest because it was out of his way did not find the pot of gold. Your work is primary, and I accept that and believe it is as it should be – for you; but that work, Cath does not have to be insulated, no painter I think has ever done that; I am overflowing with love for you and it should not sound silly when I myself write, I am somebody, you will find something in me. But I cannot give myself unless you want me, and me alone, unless you want to see whether part of me plus other forces in your life, is not very much less than all of me, alone.

'I'm not talking in the trivial terms of time, for I am not greedy for yours, Cath, and will not impose upon it as I did today.'

I should end on a light note, he reflected I should find something keen and happy, oh what foolishness, he then thought, and hastily folded the letter and sealed it.

*

While he rang the bell he repeated to himself, I will not speak about my letter; but Catherine greeted him so without any allusion to it, or to their Huguenin talk, that he was on the

174

point of asking her at least whether she had received it. He decided against it, the Swiss mail must be extremely efficient, he thought sullenly.

It was after a few words of hers that he perceived a strain under her gentle manner. 'How did you paint today?' he asked.

'I did very well,' she said, 'at least I thought so myself. I had the Lavé man here in the morning.'

He remained silent.

'He gave me a long lecture on the pursuit of art,' Catherine continued more heatedly, 'which boiled down to the profound observation that he exhibited to sell and that the painter should therefore never lose touch with his potential market.'

'I hope he –' Anthoni began, but he stopped when he saw that she had tears in her eyes. 'Catherine,' he cried, taking her hand, 'please don't let a stupid salesman in paintings upset you. Oh my dear, what is the matter with you, don't you know that this happened to everyone, including Rembrandt? These people don't know about good or bad and they don't want to know, they only care about that imaginary public taste – and taste is what was sold yesterday, never today. If he admired everything, then you should be worried –'

Catherine interrupted him. 'Yes, I know,' she said softly, 'you don't have to tell me. I'm sorry I was so silly. It's really only because he was such a pedantic ugly man, he tried to kiss my hand when he left. I have to put on some lipstick, excuse me.' She went to the bedroom.

When she came back he forgot about his intention. Her crying, his words had changed the atmosphere, and it seemed fitting to ask her what her answer to his letter would be. He was wrong. Catherine paled at his words, and then she burst out.

'Please,' she cried, 'how can I keep my mind in the middle of these tugs of war? Everybody is tugging at me, why don't they leave me alone?'

'Who is everybody, Catherine,' Anthoni asked coldly.

175

'Why, everybody, you, my mother, father, the art-dealer, Hans...'

'Is he tugging too? Does he know?'

'Of course he does. I have no secrets. If people don't approve of me they are welcome to take their leave.'

'Your reaction seems a bit out of proportion to the words I wrote you,' Anthoni said. 'I guess I'd better come back when you are calmer.' He got up, he was intending to go and Catherine saw it.

'Don't go,' she said. 'I apologize.' She smiled at him, and he looked back at her with a forced smile on his face and sat down again on the couch opposite her. He felt the blood pound in his pulses.

'I want you so, Cath,' he whispered to her in bed, 'I am so sorry, I am too – I don't know what, too nervous, I have been terribly afraid that I would not be able to make love to you, and now I really cannot.'

'Lie in my arms,' she answered, 'and let me soothe you.' He closed his eyes and did not struggle any longer against himself, and a wave of peace and sadness came over him.

'You are very precious to me, Toni,' Catherine said, 'and I do not want you to get hurt. Don't let me hurt you, but don't hurt yourself either. Perhaps I'm just a very weak woman with not enough courage to break this impasse.'

'Is it an impasse to you too then, Cath? But then, why, why can't you...?'

'Send Hans away? Oh, Toni, if you only realized how I resent this male idea of the place of a woman, this presumption that there are fundamental differences between a man and a woman in that respect ... What do I ask of you? If you desire me you may have me, for I desire you, and there is pleasure in that, and more, beauty.'

Anthoni did not answer.

*

The nebulous voyage – that was the dream of the South, it had been South America in his thought, but that was only a name, it was no country in actuality, it was an idea, a nostalgia for a place never seen, an eternally blue sky, a sunny land, with a people knowing the mysteries and not shunning them, having shaped the world without the curse and the sombreness of the North and Calvin, the beliefs born from the melancholy of November skies, grey clouds chasing across an invisible horizon, rain without end beating on the windows in the dimness of an early winter afternoon.

He had believed in the literal possibility of that geographic escape; it had been a secret reserve, he thought, he had never stopped to investigate how much of need there was in the idea, or was it all a game of his mind? Why had it lost its force, its reality as a game even, never to return, during those first days of his farming? Because of the sterility of the sun which had beaten down on him then, and which seemed to be a symbol now for the empty summer streets of waiting for Catherine? Because, half emerging, it was love which had been the essence of that dreamed country, the passion of its women, an ecstasy which would be a pain, less, senselessness without Catherine?

*

He had not asked about seeing her the next day because he had thought, I am with her too often, I need a day to catch my breath, I will want her harder and forget myself.

Yet he did go to her house that evening. For all that day he had been ever more acutely aware of the unreality of the future, of the fact that he was in Zurich only for her, so that no other ending of the void of the hours became thinkable. The town which had seemed attractive to him when he left for his farm now had the gloom of an empty theatre; even Hollandia was closed for a fortnight, the money which should last until September was more than half spent, the library – without its students, a few old men dozing over the papers, the clerk at the desk, so he imagined, looking at him with the unwanted understanding: you and me are left behind – a forbidding place.

'I was going to bed early,' Catherine said, 'but I am happy you came. Sit a bit with me, I had a lonely day. And so did you,' she suddenly went on, 'poor Toni, but you must not let yourself go like that. Why don't you use this time to finish your work?'

Anthoni shrugged. 'It bores me. I'm too restless. And after all, Cath,' he went on with a smile, 'that's not what I am here for. I am here for you.'

'Don't you have me?' Catherine asked, in a mock coquettish voice.

'I want more of you,' Anthoni could not refrain from answering, 'I wasn't being noble coming back to Zurich, I am not sacrificing myself, I am out to conquer you or be ruined. There is no attractive third choice.'

He had spoken lightly, but Catherine closed her eyes and the happiness left her face.

'Don't let me unnerve you, though,' he said, 'I won't tug, I can wait.'

'But you can't hang around in this way, it is such a waste,' Catherine remarked after a while.

'Don't worry,' he began his answer, but he stopped himself. 'Catherine,' he sighed, 'what a mess. It was all so happy, what did I spoil, where did it happen? I'm filled with the wildest premonitions . . .'

'I think you are just run down after that farm business. Why don't you go to my doctor?' Catherine said.

In the silent house the front door was heard to fall shut, and voices sounded in the corridor. Anthoni was going to answer her, but she put her hand on his to check him. She was trembling. Then she got up, knotted the cord of her dressing-gown, and murmuring: 'Please wait,' left the room, closing the door behind her.

He heard her go down the stairs, and he heard her speak, sharply. A dread suspense caught him, he opened the door and listened, then he closed it again and sat in a chair. He waited a long time, I wish I could leave, he thought, or shall I wait in her bedroom and lock the door. All had been still now for at least ten minutes.

And then he heard Catherine. She was crying, in a weird frightening way, and she was coming up the stairs. He went out into the corridor, and then he saw her coming. He felt for the wall to lean against. She was not alone. The idea crossed his mind, she looks ugly, I had never thought that possible. She was so pale that she seemed dead, her cheekbones stood out and her hair was lying dully in her face. A man supported her. 'She fainted,' he said to Anthoni, and passing him, led her into her bedroom and closed the door behind them. Her crying grew softer and stopped.

He paced up and down, stopping at the bedroom door, his hand on the knob, and retracting it again; but this is intolerable, he said to himself, 'intolerable,' he repeated aloud, that is the man then, he carries her into her bedroom, he doesn't have more right than I, God, I should go in, why didn't I feel anything seeing him, why did I just look on?

He went to the window and pressed his face against the glass and stared out into the darkness of the gardens.

He turned around when he heard the bedroom door open and close again. The man was standing in the room, and said without looking at him: 'You'd better leave. She is very over-wrought.'

Anthoni was motionless, a wild train of thought whirled through his head. Then, without answering, without turning his head, he walked out of the room, almost touching the man when he passed him, leaving the door open behind him.

In the street he thought: how odd, I would never recognize him, I have no idea how he looks. When he was at the corner he stopped and turned around and walked back to the door-way which was almost opposite her front door. He sat down on the step. There was a street lamp only a few feet to the left of him, and passers-by glanced curiously, but he did not notice it. He waited there for what must have been half an hour, and it seemed a long time to him. A man came out He was going left, and in the movement his eye caught Anthoni's. He stared at him, a second, then he lowered his look and proceeded towards Pelikan street.

Then Anthoni walked home.

*

When he opened the door of his room in the morning to go out, one of the maids from Catherine's apartment house was standing there, her hand in the air. 'I was just going to knock,' she said. 'I'm bringing you a note, sir.'

He took the blue envelope of Catherine's stationery and closed his door again, but then he hesitated and putting it in his pocket, he left the room. The maid heard him and she stopped on the bottom step of the stairs and looked back, thinking that he wanted her. He made a vague gesture and got into the elevator.

He regarded himself in the mirror while going down, and he felt the movement, the world an enormous globe, and his body proceeding towards its centre and his I was like a little man in his head, watching that. 'I'll soon be ready for the madhouse,' he told himself. He started out for his café terrace but before he reached the bridge he stopped and sat down on a bench.

'Anthoni,' he read, 'I am staying in bed today, I don't feel well and I woke up with a tormenting headache.

'I never want another evening like yesterday's for the simple reason that my body could not stand it. I regret that it happened, through no one's fault but my own, of course, and I regret that I have thus again hurt you. I have been very selfish. I think we should not see each other for some time, because I cannot accept the responsibility for a repetition. I told Hans the same. I need some time for myself and in peace. I will be lonely for you, but it has to be that way. Please don't be upset by this decision. You'll soon have to face many vital personal problems, but if you'll continue to think of me I will be happy to await you. Perhaps this letter seems preposterous to you, perhaps you have already decided that after last night you never want to see me again. I couldn't blame you. I hope you don't think of me with hatred. Your love means very much to me.'

He had stopped several times while reading, waiting for the pounding of his heart to abate, angrily shaking his head to clear the dimness of his eyes. He put the letter away, took it out and read it again. After the original terror it seemed better now. Some time, he thought, it's only for some time, I have to see her again and she will need me, she will be lonely, I will do anything, no woman is unconquerable . . . It may be then that this is the crisis which clears . . . this should be his end: why did he come to Zurich, why did she not send him away instead of me, I am more important in her life – but then she did not know, it doesn't matter, she was hysterical, the thing she needed was calmness around her, she did not let him stay the night, thanks to God, she would have done that if she had decided to choose him . . .

'My dearest one,' he wrote Catherine, 'you cannot ban me from your life for my sake, for I have no wishes but the being with you, and my desire for you is my only desire and all else I have forgotten.' Is that really true? he asked himself, but then went on writing.

'And you should not ban me for your own sake, for I have now learned my lesson, and I will discipline myself; I profess to love you and shall try to prove it that way. Tell me the lesson did not come too late and the price was not too high for you.'

The maid stepped aside after having opened the door. 'Miss

Valois is at home,' she said, 'she is resting.' He looked up those stairs and so intensely did he long for her, for the touch, the perfume of her, that he saw himself going up the steps. But he did not, and answered: 'Would you just give her this letter please?'

*

He telephoned Catherine the following noon. He had gone to the library for that, to speak to her from one of the booths in the hall. So much seemed to depend on it.

He had been apprehensive of her not answering calls, and when he heard her voice he said, 'Hello, Cath,' and then could not think of what more to say, and waited for her. She sounded lighthearted. 'Thank you for your flowers,' she said, 'they fill my room with their colour like a yellow cloud.'

'Please let me come and see you?' he whispered.

'All right,' she answered. That was all that was said.

He had sent her so many flowers that they were standing in vases all over her room. 'You look like a farmer's daughter in the pasture,' he said, and took her hand. She lifted her face to be kissed.

They undressed each other with small movements, he kissed her and lay still while she moved her body and he felt his strength ebbing and bit his lip to hold out, and then she sighed and spread her arms wide. She did not ask him about himself and he was glad for that.

'I am so happy, Catherine,' he said, 'that we, I, have a new chance. I pray that we will be wiser.'

'Let's be very simple,' she answered, 'that is even better.'

'Will you come to my place tomorrow?' he asked her.

'Tomorrow is Saturday,' she said with a sad smile at him

He looked back at her with a blank expression, but she did not speak on.

'You mean that you were lying in your letter to me?' he finally asked in a terrible voice.

She stayed very calm, she stroked his hair with a slow movement of her arm. 'No, Toni,' she answered, 'I was not lying. He insisted that he had to see me again, and I could not refuse that. I made two decisions and I broke them both. Don't make me sorry that I did.'

*

That week-end he did not go up to her house any more.

It was during the afternoon of Saturday, he was reading in his room, that he put his book down and got up to leave. All during the day he had known that he was again going to her house, to look at the closed façade and think about her with Hans, and he had let the feeling rise in him until it reached the surface and it was time to go. But as he was standing at his window, looking at the cover of the book by Proudhon with its endless title, he realized with a shock that he was blindly following an impulse from the past, that he had only been assuming he would want to go and stand opposite her house again. It is past, he thought, I don't want to do that any more. It was not a happy discovery; he had not overcome the idea, he had left it behind, and no longer felt acutely enough for that action.

He sat down again and continued reading. The weather was sunny and so blue that it seemed not possible it would ever change again, the house was still and even from the street no sound was heard, even the streetcars seemed to have stopped that long afternoon.

He went to bed while it was still light in his room, he lay on his back with his hands folded behind his head and stared at the ceiling from which the dusk light slowly withdrew and was followed by the neon colours. He had given in to a sadness now and had peace in it, a bottomless sadness, not wholly explained; was it all and only because of Catherine, he thought, because he knew now that she would never be one with him, that he was refused?

On Sunday night he had just fallen asleep when he was

183

awakened by the telephone ringing in the pension. It was a little sound through the two doors, and he closed his eyes again, but the telephone persisted. There was nobody at home to answer. Three more rings, he thought, and at the fourth he got up and went to answer it. It was Catherine, and he was strangely not surprised.

'I'd like to see you,' she said, 'Can I come over?'

'Yes, of course,' Anthoni replied, and added, 'Should I come and get you?'

'No, I'll come now.'

He went quickly back to his room, put on the light next to the bed, straightened things, regarded himself again and again in the mirror. After a quarter of an hour he grew calmer and lay down on his bed. Soon after she came.

He kissed her and made her sit down and told her how happily she had surprised him and he thought I am not very glad, I could almost say I would rather have dreamed about her, alone.

'I'm unwell,' Catherine said, 'but if you'll have me I want to stay with you tonight.'

They did not speak about the preceding two days. She said that she wanted to look at him for a long time; there was a feverishness in her which caught him, and she kissed him in a torture until he had it, but she continued, looking down upon him, moving herself against him, 'I feel like a Bacchante,' she said, and he received her storm, passively almost, again, up to a state of being utterly spent.

But he remained lying awake, until the morning, when he insisted on seeing her home, putting on his shoes, trousers, and a raincoat; and returned to his room to fall on his bed almost unconscious and sleep the day through.

*

The landlady was closing her front door when he came out the following morning, and on seeing him she opened it again. 'Perhaps we can settle the rent since I am here anyway,' she said. 'Are you afraid that I'll run away?' he asked sharply, 'it's just the first of the month – I don't like being jumped upon in a corridor, I have no time now.' He slapped the elevator button with his fist and when nothing happened stamped down the stairs without looking back at her.

He was shaking, I am going to pieces, he thought, and moved by a compulsion he walked with big steps down to Catherine's house and pressed the bell. He had never been there at that time of the morning.

When he saw Catherine, looking very prim with her hair tied back, her hand black with charcoal, he hesitated. She frowned, annoyed, and the force in him caught him again. 'Catherine,' he said in a trembling voice, 'I know I shouldn't interrupt you, I never will again, but I couldn't start another day like this ... I want you, I want you to marry me ... and if you won't, I want you to swear that you will be faithful to me – just these few weeks till I'm leaving for the war – you must do it, you can't leave me with my thoughts ... they madden me ...'

Catherine threw her coal on the floor, and then she snatched her drawing from the easel and began to tear it up. 'It's no use,' she cried, 'I give up.'

Anthoni jumped up and held her by her wrists, and she dropped the pieces. He stooped and picked them up, and stood there, looking at them with a struck face.

'I'm sorry I changed my mind,' she now said softly. 'We make each other suffer needlessly. I can't swear those things, Toni. I don't want to belong. Don't ask me another time.'

'Forgive me for this scene,' Anthoni answered slowly. 'It will not happen any more. You won't see me again.'

He walked out of the room and into the street, not seeing anything, tears running down his face, holding the pieces of her drawing in both hands.

To the river, and then he walked along the embankment he did not know how long, but he felt more and more weary, and then he sat down on the steps of a house, and he took the funicular, Hollandia had reopened that day and he went there without knowing why, remaining standing at the door. Ernst looked up at him from behind the counter with a serious face, meeting his eyes, and said: 'I have a message for you from Iel, your farmer. He called already last week.' Anthoni accepted the note. 'Shall we settle accounts today?' Ernst asked. 'I will be back.' He heard Ernst whisper to his wife while he opened the door and left. 'The inspector comes the first of August,' the note said, 'it might be safer for you to be here one day.' Without thinking further he threw the note in the street and walked down to the station. He was still holding her drawing clutched in his left hand, and he looked around him, the houses will jump on me, he said to himself, am I play-acting or am I losing my mind? It was noon when he entered the station. The next train for Lucerne left at two-thirty and he bought a ticket and sat down on a bench. So much noise, what am I doing here, why all these pursuits, why do they run to catch a train? He got up from his bench. He looked at the newspapers, I have to touch an 'A', he thought, quickly. His heart was beating so fast that it dimmed his hearing. He left the station again and came out in the square. I can't do this, he thought, I can't go to Lucerne, I will go to Geneva, and try to cross the border tonight. I must see Jean-Pierre first. He began to walk towards Day's hotel. His panic did not diminish. Let's stop a minute, he said to himself. No, I can't go to Day. I don't want to go to the war any more. I am lost.

He thought of himself and he choked, he thought of all his plans and ideas and felt so sorry, so endlessly regretting, that he leaned his face against the wall of the houses and held himself with trembling hands.

He went on, but he passed the side street to the hotel where Day lived. How strange, he thought, I'll never see Day again, that confused hour was the last time ... and all the money I borrowed, I hope ... He would never see him again. He knew now, and he looked ahead over the sun-baked Bahnhof street, and he shuddered without stopping. He was going home to kill himself. His shaking would not end, and his teeth chattered. 'It'll stop,' he murmured, 'it'll stop.'

More about Penguins
and Pelicans

Penguinews, which appears every month, contains details of all the new books issued by Penguins as they are published. From time to time it is supplemented by *Penguins in Print*, which is a complete list of all available books published by Penguins. (There are some five thousand of these.)

A specimen copy of *Penguinews* will be sent to you free on request. For a year's issues (including the complete lists) please send 50p if you live in the United Kingdom, or 75p if you live elsewhere. Just write to Dept EP, Penguin Books Ltd, Harmondsworth, Middlesex, enclosing a cheque or postal order, and your name will be added to the mailing list.

Note: *Penguinews* and *Penguins in Print* are not available in the U.S.A. or Canada

H. E. Bates

Fair Stood the Wind for France

'*Fair Stood the Wind for France* is perhaps the
finest novel of the war . . . The scenes are
exquisitely done and the characters – tenderly
and beautifully drawn – are an epitome of all
that is best in the youth of the two countries.
This is a fine, lovely book which makes the
heart beat with pride'

– *Daily Telegraph*

Not for sale in the U.S.A.

Graham Greene

The End of the Affair

This frank, intense account of a love-affair and its mystical aftermath is set in a suburb of London, and told with the intimate informality of the first person. The story tells of the strange and callous steps taken by a middle-aged writer to destroy – or perhaps to reclaim – the mistress who had unaccountably left him eighteen months before.

'For me one of the most true and moving novels of my time, in anybody's language'
– William Faulkner

Not for sale in the U.S.A.